READERS,

MANY THANKS FOR
YOUR SUPPORT AND KEEP
DREAMING THOSE DREAMS —

AUGUST
2025

DREAMS OF DARKNESS DREAMS OF NIGHT

20TH ANNIVERSARY EDITION

TERRY D. SCHEERER

www.darkmythpublications.com

Dark Myth Publications
145 S Glenoaks Blvd.
Unit #3149,
Burbank, CA 91502

ISBN: 979-8-9925038-4-5
First Printing August 2025

Dark Myth Publications is a registered trademark of The JayZoMon Dark Myth Company, LLC.

10 9 8 7 6 5 4 3 2 1

Printing History:

- *Between the Moon and Mars, A Lasting Relationship* and *Falling* appeared in the September, 2004 issue of The World of Myth.

- *Death Chant* and *Succubus* appeared in the October, 2004 issue o The World of Myth.

- *Darkness Falls* and *Love Is...* appeared in the November, 2004 issue of The World of Myth.

- *All Gone, The Eater of Dreams, Final Question* and an abridged version of *Silent Screams* appeared in the December, 2004 issue of The World of Myth.

- To Dance with the Dead was serialized in the January, February and March, 2005 issues of The World of Myth.

Books by Terry D. Scheerer:

- **The Dragon Hunters and Other Fantasy Tails** – Dark Myth Publications – 2011

Other works by Terry D. Scheerer:

- The World of Myth Anthology Vol.3 – All That Glitters/It's Later Than You Think – Dark Myth Publications – 2018

- Zombie EPICdemic – Why do Zombies eat People – Zombie Works Publications – 2018
- The World of Myth Anthology Vol.2 – The Squid Kid – Dark Myth Publications – 2010
- The World of Myth Anthology Vol.1 – Adrift/Dead and Ferried – Dark Myth Publications – 2007

For Buddy and Wendy and all those gone ahead,
out of the Darkness and into the Light.

Table of Contents

Table of Contents (Cont'd)

FOREWORD

I needed to revisit this book before I sat down to write this. I spent most of the day consuming his words allowing them to draw images of tales that he dreamed up in his mind to only to be shared with us the reader. As each scene fades into my mind's eye and fade to the next, it left me with a feeling that I would get when waking from a dream and remembering it, as if it stuck to your soul somehow.

I had read his words many times, in my younger years I actually studied them as he was my mentor and taught me how to craft a short story, but this time the words hit different. It was something that I did not realize as twenty-something, his words lingered like when you look into a mirror and you see something you have seen many times, but there was something new this time. So you stared and focused on it until you figure out what the difference was.

This book. His poems. His stories.

They were a mirror into the man, his confessional, if you will. I'm not talking Terry D. Scheerer, the author that we all knew and loved, but the human being. The man he was when doors were closed and the people weren't caring. This publication *Dreams of Darkness, Dreams of Night* was an autobiography told through factious narrative, about the journey of one man who wrestled with shadows that most of us spend a lifetime trying to avoid.

In all the years I knew Terry, not once did he ever ask if I liked a piece, because he didn't write to impress me, or anyone who read his work to be honest. He wrote because he *had* to! Every story, every poem especially in this collection is drenched in the weight of real life experience, that of loss, of disappointment, of love barely held and so too often lost.

But unlike most who deal with those real life situations, Terry was defiant. In his words a voice that was heard, "Even if the world doesn't make sense, I'm still here. I'm still telling the story."

What made Terry stand out to me was how he never ran from the hard stuff. He looked life straight in the face and wrote what he felt, no filters, no fancy language to cover it up. What he put on the page was real, raw, honest, and exactly how he saw it.

In this moment, what you hold in your hand is the anniversary of the raw, honest product of a man who squared off with life and chose to write it down, no matter how dark things got. Trust me, he carried more than his fair share of *darkness*.

If you were lucky enough to have known Terry on a personal level, you knew his sense of humor, his sharp mind, and the way he could turn anything into an idea for a story and twist it just enough to make the reader slightly uneasy.

You also knew the pain behind his smile, and that's all here in these pages. Every hidden fear, every fragile hope he carried is woven into the work. So take your time with it. Let the words settle in. This isn't just fiction. You're stepping into Terry's world.

Into his dreams. Into his night.

If you come out of this *dark ride* on the other side a little more aware of your own darkness, well, I think that's exactly what he'd hoped for.

David K. Montoya
Chief Executive Officer & Publisher,
The JayZoMon Dark Myth Company, LLC.

INTRODUCTION

Welcome aboard and thank you for stopping by. A few years ago on a television sitcom, an actor played the night manager of a bus terminal in a run down, seedy section of a mid-western city. In his small, dingy office, the walls were devoid of any personal effects, save one. Behind his desk there hung a small sign, which he supposedly had pilfered from some carney as a young man. That sign read: "This is a DARK ride". He kept that sign hanging where he could see it every night to remind him that 'Life' itself was sometimes a ride with a very dark side.

The journey you are about to embark upon may also be considered a 'dark ride'. The work included in this volume spans some thirty-five years of my life-much of which (to me, at least) appeared to be dark, dismal, depressing and without hope. Such, I have been led to believe, frequently and also unfortunately, is life.

While many of the poems contained herein were penned during two especially traumatic periods during the past two and a half decades, the stories, except for one, were all written in the past four or five years, after moving to the barren, desolate wasteland that is the Southern California High Desert. And, even though my life has not actually been a constant, swirling vortex of nightmares and darkness-it only seems that way, sometimes-the work in this book speaks of the pain and torment many people have suffered through, most often in a fragile, painful silence.

It is not all death and destruction, however, as a few of the stories do have a positive ending-well, one or two of them, anyway. But, each poem and every story in this book contains a fragment of my life; some of the tears, the pain, the loss and the fear that I have experienced over the years.

These things are all quite real. It is frequently said that a writer should write about what he (or she) knows and if what they are most familiar with is death, pain and suffering, then what other words should come from their pens?

So, it's just about time to start. Please remember to keep your hands and arms inside the ride at all times (you never know what might be lurking out there in the shadows) and remain seated until the car has come to a complete stop.

Good luck and I hope you enjoy your ride to a curious and perhaps demented place, which you may sometimes have to pass through, but where you would never want to stay.

Terry D. Scheerer
Hesperia, California
April, 2005

DREAMS OF DARKNESS DREAMS OF NIGHT

20TH ANNIVERSARY EDITION

For the moon is the mother of all lunatics
and so they are given
Her name.

—*Unknown*

Dreams of Darkness

Poems

Concert for None

On a barren hill
Two graves are standing
There joined forever.

The headstones are cold
The graves are covered with dust
And no one came to mourn.

One Death

...for Clemmie Wilson
July, 1971

Waiting in the white-black silence
As life's last breath gasps past quivering lip
A soul escapes earthbound bondage with a sigh
To soar now free, to float on high.

Search

I must seek to end this painful existence
There is no joy to behold in the land
Tumors grow in cancerous riot in the womb of my mind
Only agony is clear
My dreams show me the way
To travel inward to the mind's eye
There, visions abound
Nightmares that race the wind
Soundless screams fill the void
Death is there to line my path
To tell me there is no peace in life.

TERRY D. SCHEERER

The Light Fails

My world is shrouded in darkness
A black stain creeps slowly across my soul
Leprous, it assaults my senses
Driving me down
Down into the fetid depths of my being
There, I wander, forever lost
Lost amidst my dreams
Seeking refuge from the numbing pain
That is my life.

Falling

Help me, I'm falling
From the height of my despair
To the depth of my depression
Falling
In slow motion spirals
To the darkness below.

Screaming, without sound
I am beset by creatures of my dreams
Monsters, bred of my tear
This fallacy of life
Stifles, corrupts, destroys
Then devours the spirit.

Into the vortex, plunge
Falling

TERRY D. SCHEERER

Surrounded by fragments of terror
These beings of my dread
Snatch away my sanity
Pain encompasses my soul
And it is gone-torn away on the howling wind
Falling, forever falling.

...for all those I have known who shall forever be...

Useless

Time is not
Love contaminated
Life merely was
Useless.
Mind dreams
Contorted visions dance
To a Death Head's
Laughter
Useless...
      As time
        As love
          As life.

Love is...

Love is a flower that grows from a seed,
Nurtured by need, then killed by greed.
The color is red, from the blood that is shed,
On love it once fed, yet soon to be dead.
We were a flower, you and I,
Just waiting for our love to die—
For the bud in full bloom, was surrounded by gloom.
Our petals have fallen to lie on the ground,
A pale reflection of our intense affection.
The stem that was mine now withers on the vine,
Turning brown and dried, in pain it has died.
And as my life has gone before,
Seek to let my spirit soar,
In hopes that death is not merely...

The End

Final Question

I am poised upon a pillar tall,
Just waiting for the coming fall.
High above the land and sea,
Knowing it's too late for me.
Yesterdays will tell the tale,
Always close, but always fail.
Tried so hard to reach the top,
Now, it's just a longer drop.
All around see the signs,
Time to cut the tie that binds.
Too late now to change the past,
Almost time to take the leap,
To lay me down and finally sleep.
But, before I go, I need to know,
Why doesn't anything rhyme with orange?

TERRY D. SCHEERER

A Lasting Relationship

On a vast, windswept shore
I mourn, oh, no more
For the love that now I've lost
and of what may be the cost.

Love's trust once more is broken
With words but a fleeting token
Of things that were so softly said
Amid hidden pleasures within our bed.

Thus, I have set firm my mind
And now, hope but to find
In my death, the one true friend
That may be faithful, until the end

Going Home

...for Edgar A. Poe

The cool, quiet darkness
Comforts, soothes, protects.
Surrounded by the blackened void
The softness swells, to encompass the whole.
The peace infinite
The quiet eternal
The darkness forever.
The pain of life is fleeting, minor;
A mere step on the path of a longer journey.

Floating in that sea of tranquility
Throughout eternity, protected,
Quiet, serene within the darkness.
Death is the constant companion;
The ever faithful mate.

TERRY D. SCHEERER

We are born, but to die,
Starting far away and moving slowly toward
Our ultimate goal: the eternal womb.
We must all go home someday.
For some, the journey is longer than others—
For some, so short as to go unnoticed.
To go home, to be within the peace of Death.
To go home, once again.

Succubus

Cold and dark as death she doth creep,
    o'er land and hearth and home.
She steals away the warmth of day,
    to seek wherein the dreamers lay.

With light caress—a kiss no less,
    she *sucks* men void of life,
Then leaves behind an empty shell
    and thus sated, returns to Hell!

TERRY D. SCHEERER

Burning Bright

Once upon a clear, dark night,
    when the stars were, oh, so bright,
I thought I saw a shooting star
    and wondered, 'Had it traveled very far?'

Such a tiny bit of space debris,
    come all this way for me to see —
A million miles of dark and cold,
    through space and time to be this old.

I shed a tear to see it die,
    against the velvet darkness of the sky.
A flaming trail, burning bright,
    once upon a clear, dark night.

The Eater of Dreams

...for H.P. Lovecraft

Beneath a storm-laced, blood red sky,
On a desolate, wind-swept shore,
The Nameless One doth in agony, lie.

For untold eons he hath lain in wait—
Only leaving this nocturnal strand
When some poor mortal calls open the gate.

But, then can his leprous wings take flight,
As he soars o'er the realm of darkened dreams
To travel through time and pitch black night.

Thus, to slacken his hunger and finally feed
On the dreams of those who unknowingly called
The Nameless One, that he can fulfill a dreadful
need.

17

TERRY D. SCHEERER

Silent Screams

Silent screams, echoes of fright,
Empty voices fill the night.

All around I hear the cries,
Of tormented souls, with sightless eyes.

Lost and forlorn, ne'er more to be free,
These spirits of the Damned call out to me.

And what do they say when they talk to me so?
They tell me to leave, that it's time to go.

These voices I hear, those silent screams,
Cry out that life is not at all what it seems.

We have one chance in Hell to do this up right,

Else we too will be just silent screams, lost in the night.

All Gone

My life seems a wasted effort, no matter how hard I
try;
Looks like the only solution is to lie down and die.
The voices I hear keep egging me on,
But if I do what they want, I'll just be a pawn.
So I'll do what 'I' want and to Hell with them all!
This should be fun, at least 'til my fall.
Then the pieces of my life will be all swept away,
And will I be remembered fondly? Well, maybe,
some day.
It might be better if I had family or friends,
Someone to talk to and thus make amends.
But now it seems that I'm all on my own—
Sure, I have 'people' around, but I still feel alone.
Worthless and shattered, I just can't go on,
Will anyone even notice, when I am gone?

Spirit Dog

...for Buddy
February 16, 2004

If a good and gentle pet were to sicken and die,
Who would stand by his side, to thus say goodbye?
In this world he knew people, but only we three,
And in the end, at his grave, it was just Pongo and
me.
I laid him to rest in winter, 'neath a tree bare of
growth,
But, on his anniversary, spring buds had come forth.
Life renewed, full circle, had come to the tree;
He's gone now, at peace, may his spirit run free.
Now he can chase rabbits and birds all through the
day,
Or in the tall grass, with his paws up, he might lay.
Dear Buddy, may your loving spirit run forever free,
I'm just sorry that you are no longer here, with me.
You were a special gift, which I shall always miss,

21

TERRY D. SCHEERER

Fare thee well, dear friend, to a better place than this.

Good boy, Buddy. Good boy!

Last Sunrise

We died at dawn, Buddy and me,
Together, beneath that cold, winter tree.
I laid him to rest with a pillow for his head,
If only They had taken me, instead.
Now he's gone and I'm still here,
But not a day goes by that I don't shed a tear.
A part of me died too, on that cold winter dawn,
It's still so hard to believe that he is gone.
Why would They take a soul so gentle and kind?
It's not as if wretched souls were that hard to find
But, they chose to make an angel of this good and
true friend,
And I'll hate Them for that, until my own final end.
The only consolation I have in this mind-numbing
fog,
Is that god, spelled backwards, will always be *DOG*.

23

TERRY D. SCHEERER

Why I Cry

I cry for time lost, never to regain
And I cry, now, to simply ease my pain.
I cry because I miss your great furry face—
Others may come and go,
But shall never take your place.
I cry because they took away my one, true friend,
One who loved me, unconditionally,
Until the very end.

Darkness Falls

Darkness is falling and I'm too tired to fight,
I can hear them calling—spirits lost in the night.
These creatures of the dark feed off of my mind,
I should have been safe, but they seek their own
kind.

They hunt me amid the chaos of my dreams,
My sleep is now haunted by nightmares and
screams.
A riderless horse crawls by on its knees,
I 'have' asked for help, but they do as they please.

I can't fight this battle alone any more,
I'm not even sure what I am living for.
The war is now lost, I'm a causality of life,
I can't continue amid all this stress and strife.

TERRY D. SCHEERER

I am constantly beset by my anger and fears,
My only companions are these frequent tears.
If he were still with me, where would I be?
I'm trapped here and he's gone, but now at least
free.

I've tried to be strong, but it's too much to bear,
And who ever said, "Life has to be fair?"
I have done what I can, but now I know,
I'm all by myself, so it's time to go.

The damage is done, there's too much to mend,
So, it's finally time to just say...

The End

Dreams of Night

Short Stories

To Dance with the Dead

This story was written some years after my own grandmother passed away, unexpectedly, in July, 1971. She helped raise me while my mother worked and attended college and I have many fond memories of our time spent together. While a good many aspects of the following story are based on fact, I borrowed the style-first person narrative-from the famous horror writer of the 1930s, Howard Phillips Lovecraft. The descriptions of the mausoleum are all true and accurate; I spent many hours wandering the cool, quiet halls and corridors of that huge necropolis after my grandmother was entombed there, and the actual idea for this story was born somewhere in the deep, underground crypt described in the later pages. How much of this story is truth and how much is merely fiction? Well, I'll let you decide that for yourself, after you have read...

To Dance with the Dead

...for Clemmie Wilson
January 25, 1894 - July 23, 1971

WHILE ANY WHO know me personally, know of my near solitary background and untoward habits may attempt to pass off what I have to tell as a mere dream fantasy, or a nightmare perhaps brought about by my intense grief and an overly active imagination, I assure you that what I have to tell did, in fact, take place.

It was my beloved grandmother, now gone from me forever, whose departure from this unkind world started me on my unexpected nightmare journey. As I was orphaned at an early age, it was this wonderful and gentle woman who took me into her home and to her heart, showering me with more love and kindness than I would have ever thought humanly possible.

While I am sure that my parents did, in fact, love me in their own way, at the time of their death in an auto accident, they had been too busy leaving their mark on

31

the world to spare much of an outward show of affection on a pale, sickly four year old. My grandmother, on the other hand, seemed to have all the time in the world and for many happy years she unselfishly shared her love and her life with me.

She was fortunately blessed with the patience of a saint, a virtue she sorely required in order to deal with me during those early years we spent together. For shortly after my third birthday, I developed a case of asthma that soon reached the chronic stage. As a result of this recurring malady, I was required to stay indoors much of the time during my formative years and had only my grandmother to act as both companion and playmate.

As I was frequently bedridden due to my bouts of asthma—not to mention my other sundry illnesses— my grandmother would often spend a good part of her own day playing different card and board games with me. Then, in the evening, before tucking me into bed, she would unfailingly read to me from classic tales of fantasy and imagination, no doubt in an attempt to turn my thoughts away from my own personal problems and at the same time to perhaps spark within me an interest in the world of literature.

In the latter respect, at least, she was highly successful. I soon longed to read for myself of the places, times and people she had introduced me to and with her assistance, at an early age I was able to find increasing solace from my illness plagued and lonely world in my late grandfather's well stocked library. As I grew older, I would while away countless hours reading and daydreaming of mysterious and ofttimes horrific far off places and of journeys through other times and dimensions as described within the pages of books by such authors as Edgar Allan Poe, Robert E. Howard and H.P. Lovecraft.

Basically left for the most part to my own devices to amuse myself over the years, it is no small wonder that my thoughts were turned inward and I tended more and more to rely on literary fantasy and my own imagination to fill the void left in my life by the lack of normal outside stimulus. By the age of twelve I was hopelessly addicted to tales of fantasy and horror, the macabre and the supernatural. I would often spend entire days with King Kull in Valusia, with Bran Mak Morn or perhaps the great Conan as they battled their bloody way across ancient lands populated by demons, sorcerers and beautiful princesses.

But, it was during the long and lonely nights that I did the reading that excited my imagination the most—that which filled me with a deep and lingering terror that I both loved and feared. Often reading into the waning hours of the night, those pages of my book illuminated by the flickering glow of a single candle flame (I used a candle to read by at night for just a bit of melodramatic atmosphere—I felt it only fitting to read such books in as much of a sympathetic surrounding as possible), I would thus wander the decaying, deserted streets of Innsmouth, prowl the dreary hills and woods outside Arkham, seek after vampires and demons or visit ghoul haunted graveyards and moldering castles by the score.

TERRY D. SCHEERER

Often as not, after such a night of reading, I would awaken in the early morning hours, crying aloud from some unspeakable nightmare. Then, inevitably, my grandmother would appear, to sit on the edge of my bed and sooth me with quiet, comforting words and gentle strokes of my hair. She would always assure me that everything would be all right, that nothing could harm me while she was there to watch over me and would then sit with me until I fell into a peaceful sleep.

Throughout those early years, I read voraciously and by the time I was fifteen, I had all but exhausted the available literature by my favorite authors and to further amuse myself, I began to write my own stories of fantasy and horror. I invented my own magical realms and peopled them with strong, valiant heroes and beautiful, fair damsels, often as not beset by evil witches, vile demons or hideous monsters. I wrote of living corpses, of unseen creatures that would devour the minds and souls of men, of secret societies that worshiped long forgotten demons and who would then summon them from the abyss to roam the darkest nights. My now fertile imagination poured forth such stories by the score.

About this time, too, as my health permitted, I began to take long walks about the city and surrounding countryside, much as Poe and Lovecraft did in their own time. I would visit local cemeteries by the hour, often using the time spent therein to write out story lines or merely to daydream about the hundreds of silent souls lying in eternal repose within the earth. On other days, I might seek out old, abandoned and neglected houses in search of story material or merely to revel in the ancient, decaying atmosphere these forgotten structures embodied. Later on, I began to undertake trips of longer duration, always carrying with me my camera and notebook to capture and retain such thoughts and pictures that might eventually end up as material for a future story.

My dear grandmother not only indulged my fancies and hobbies, but faithfully supported and encouraged me, both in my writing endeavors and in my sightseeing and information gathering trips. Never once, in all those years did her love and affection lag or diminish.

It was therefore with deep shock that after fifteen years of unfailing love and support, this one person I truly cared for should die so suddenly from a devastating stroke. I was nearly prostrate with grief at this unexpected tragedy but, as I was her only living relative, the awesome task of the funeral preparations fell heavily upon my shoulders. For the next three days then, I had little or no rest, such did my grief and the exhausting burden of the burial arrangements tell on me. Though I loathe to admit it, it was actually with something akin to relief when all was finally arranged and we took my dear grandmother to be entombed on the afternoon of February 1st.

During the services, I found myself drifting; thinking back to that one other funeral I had attended, so many years now gone. Being as young as I was at the time, I had not understood at all what was actually taking place. I had been informed that it was my mother and father lying there, sleeping in those funny looking, boxlike beds and that they were going to heaven and I would never see them again. But, I knew that was a lie. Those big, ugly dolls didn't even look like my parents (I learned much later that both of their faces had required quite a bit of cosmetic restoration to enable the open casket viewing). I was sure that my mother and father were just away on another of their frequent business trips and would be coming home any day now with presents for me, just as they had always done before.

I had been, for the most part, rather bored and sleepy during the service, wondering vaguely why so many people around me were silently crying. But, when I was taken forward by my paternal grandparents and told to kiss those dolls goodbye, with everyone watching me while looking so solemn and expectant, I became frightened. I was lifted up by my grandfather and he leaned me over the open casket so I could kiss this thing that he claimed was my father. I tried to grab onto the edge of the casket and push myself away from that horror, but my small hands slipped and I tipped forward, my head cracking into the face of the corpse.

In utter panic, I tried frantically to push myself away from the coffin. My hands landed on the head and chest of thing within, the body being hard in places and nauseatingly soft and yielding in others. As I pushed against its face, the lips were pulled back to reveal blackened gums surmounting broken and jagged teeth. I could see where the jaw had been wired shut to prevent it falling open at an inopportune moment and a foul, sickly sweet odor wafted up to me. I was screaming hysterically by this time, my fear being intensified by the fact that the face had partially caved in where my hands had pushed in the embalmer's putty, leaving ragged, bloodless gaps in the pale, powdered flesh.

Finally, my dear grandmother—she who had been against my attending this funeral from the very beginning—managed to snatch me from the arms of my paternal grandfather and rushed me out of the church, while I sobbed brokenly against her breast. I experienced horrible nightmares for months following that incident, reliving in my dreams the entire episode —except in my dreams the corpses became animated, rising out of their coffins with spasmodic, jerking movements. Their bodies lurched to the floor and began to chase me through endless darkened corridors, my father's face misshapen and broken, with portions of his skull showing whitely through skin that had turned a sickly, leprous green.

I ran screaming through the corridors of my dreams, my short legs pumping madly, but seemingly moving me not at all. The bodies of my parents stayed close behind me, their rotting flesh dripping from their decomposing corpses in putrefying blobs with every step they took. I could smell the overpowering stench of their bodies becoming stronger as they closed the gap between us and just as I felt a claw like, bony hand grip my shoulder, I would wake up, crying in terror. That was the start of my grandmother's sitting up with me following my soon to be frequent nightmares, comforting and protecting me then, as she was to do for so many years to come.

Not wishing this funeral to resemble in any way that earlier, nightmarish experience, my grandmother's casket was closed during her service. I wanted to remember her the way she had been—full of life and love—not pale, cold and made up to look like a parody of herself.

She was laid to her final rest at Green Meadows Mausoleum, an imposing, three story edifice built in the early 1920s. The interior was extremely impressive; columned, walled and floored with variegated marble in black, green, pink and white. Many of the inner corridors seemed to stretch away endlessly, the walls tiered to receive as many as five caskets, one atop the other, from floor to ceiling. It was so cool, quiet and peaceful within the walls of that gigantic tomb that under other, less tragic circumstances, I could have wandered about the place for many hours.

There were few mourners to stand with me in my time of grief. We had no other relatives and grandmother had been so busy caring for our home and for me these past years that she rarely had time for outside social functions or for keeping up with but a few friends, while I myself had literally no one whom I could have called a friend. The church service was thankfully uneventful and the minister said but a few words prior to the actual entombment, as throughout the service I had been feeling increasingly faint and dizzy; the emotional trauma of the past few days finally beginning to take its toll on me.

After the others had passed their condolences to me one final time and quietly slipped away, I slumped down, suddenly exhausted, on a marble bench across from grandmother's flower bedecked casket and lost myself in thought. Amid the silent, meandering memories of the time spent with my grandmother, I seemed to feel the presence of a thousand sleeping souls pressing in on my conscience.

I was gradually becoming more and more weary as I sat in that quiet tomb and the cloying scent of the flowers before me had begun to make my head swim. I rose to my feet and surprised myself by staggering slightly so that I had to catch my balance by leaning against the near wall for a moment. I realized that my fatigue was now obviously draining away my limited resources of strength and steadying myself, I went in search of someplace to perhaps splash a bit of cool water on my face.

At the end of the corridor, nearly hidden from view, I found an alcove wherein a small door labeled 'Flower Room' was located. Opening the door, I discovered a room no larger than an average closet, illuminated by a bare bulb of low wattage. Inside was a small sink and several long handled poles used for inserting vases of flowers into the round receiving rings of the higher crypts, along with an assortment of the conical shaped vases for the flowers to be placed in.

Entering the tiny room, I gratefully closed the door behind me and turned on the tap over the sink to let the water run cool. I allowed the water to wash over my hands and wrists for a moment, then with some wet paper towels, I dabbed at my sticky forehead and temples, relishing the cool dampness. Turning off the tap, I leaned back against the wall, pressed the moist towels over my eyes and slowly slipped down into a sitting position, my back against the cool marble. Alone now, my duty to my grandmother finished, I finally let my grief escape. Resting my head on my knees, I wept silent tears and though not actively religious, I nevertheless prayed to whatever god there might be for the gentle soul of my departed one.

# # #

I awoke, much to my surprise and alarm, still crouched in that small flower room, my muscles much stiffened by long and cramped immobility. I looked at my watch and was shocked by the time—it was after ten o'clock. I had somehow allowed my fatigued body to cajole me into sleeping for nearly six hours! Lurching to my feet amid pinprick attacks of re-circulation in my legs, I flung open the door onto a darkened hallway.

I stood there for a moment, holding to the door frame for support, then voiced a tentative, "Hello?" The sound of my voice echoed hollowly down the dark passage without answer. The silence of that night black tomb seemed broken only by the hammering of my terrified heart. Reeling back into the flower room, I turned on the tap over the sink and splashed cold water on my face, both to help shock the sleep from my mind and to try and calm my growing fear. Cupping my hands under the flow of water, I drank several times, trying in vain to quench a sudden thirst and an unnatural dryness of my throat.

Calmed only slightly, I braced my hands against the cold, hard porcelain of the sink and tried to take stock of my situation. What had happened seemed painfully obvious. My exhaustion must have overcome me as I crouched in that out of the way room and as I blissfully slept, I was apparently overlooked when the mausoleum was closed for the night. Now, it appeared that I would have to attempt to arouse a watchman or failing in that, try to find my own way out. The thought, however, of wandering through that maze of darkened corridors, surrounded on all sides by the recumbent dead sent a new shiver of terror through me. For even though I might, at times, revel in the exploration of ancient graveyards and moldering tombs, and could both read and pen tales of crawling horror which depicted acts of the walking dead, the actuality of my present situation brought back my childhood fears of the dead crashing to the forefront of my mind.

Forcing down my fear somewhat, I turned off the water, dried my face and hands and then steeling myself, took a cautious step into the corridor. Beyond where the light fell from the just quitted room, there seemed only blackness. I attempted to call out once again, but my voice unexpectedly cracked, the resulting sound much like the cry of some small, stricken animal. That squeaking echo, as it reverberated off the marble walls, quelled me to silence.

Knowing that the only way I would be able to find an exit was to begin looking for one, I willed myself to take a few tentative steps into the darkness. My most immediate problem in attempting to locate a way out was the fact that I was completely lost in that labyrinth of the dead. I knew for certain only that I was somewhere on the third floor of the mausoleum, but any sense of direction I might have possessed was totally obliterated due to the pervading blackness.

Moving reluctantly away from the light given forth from the flower room, I proceeded slowly, one hand trailing lightly along the marble wall. My fingers began to occasionally slide over incised lettering—the sealed doorway of some soul's final bed. I was already trembling badly and began to snatch my hand quickly away from the wall whenever I encountered those etchings in the stone. I seemed to have the rather hysterical feeling that if I touched those names carved into the marble, the cadaver within would somehow know I was out here and would thus take offense at my presence. In my mind's eye, I could see the moldering corpses sitting up within their rotting caskets (much as I had dreamed I saw my own father's corpse do), pounding and clawing at the hard marble that imprisoned them; trying to get out, trying to reach me.

Fighting down a growing sense of panic, I began to shuffle forward more rapidly and when my foot encountered an unseen obstacle on the floor, I stumbled and lost my balance. Try as I might, my frantic hands could find no purchase on the slick stone wall and crying out in terror filled fright, I fell to the floor with a seemingly deafening crash. Fumbling desperately to regain my feet, my hands came upon a mass of soft and yielding material, from which cold, slimy liquid oozed as I pressed down on it. My fear was now such that I was sure I had stumbled over a recently loosed, decaying corpse and I quickly jerked my hand away from the object I had touched.

But even as that mad thought was racing through my mind, my nose informed me of the true identity of the unseen mess beneath me and I discovered that I had been struggling helplessly amid a pile of slightly wilted and now severely crushed flowers. Forcing down a feeling of laughter welling up inside of me at the spectacle I must have presented (if there had been anyone to witness it), I realized I had merely come across the flowers left by myself and the other mourners at my own grandmother's entombment earlier in the day.

Leaning back against the wall, I tried to catch my breath and collect my thoughts. Knowing for the moment, at least, that I was safe, I hoped that the terrible racket I had made as I fell would perhaps draw the attention of a custodian to my presence. But, strain as I might, I could discern no sound other than my own somewhat labored breathing.

Feeling a bit forlorn at my not be rescued, I was also saddened by the knowledge that just a few feet above my head, my dear one was now locked away, to spend eternity in a narrow stone box. And yet, even in death, she had managed to help me in my time of need, for I now had some idea as to my location and knew that if I continued moving along this corridor, I should soon arrive at the central hall. From that point, I could take the stairs down to the main floor and hence, to an exit.

As I thought of that sweet, gentle soul once again coming to my aid, tears began to well up in my eyes and as I tried to wipe them away, I found I was still holding a small bunch of crushed flowers clutched tightly in my hand. I set the flowers down as gently as possible amid the unseen wreckage I had caused, then wiped my face and slowly regained my feet. Looking up into the darkness above me, I silently thanked my grandmother for her help and then prayed for added strength to see me safely through this ordeal.

Somewhat sobered by the thought that she was still somehow watching over me, I continued my journey down the corridor, the wall just brushing my left shoulder as I walked. Shortly, I was able to discern a feeble glow of light some distance ahead of me and I had to restrain myself from rushing headlong toward that meager spot of brightness. Maintaining my slow advance, I came to a point where the wall could no longer be felt against my shoulder. I put my hand out to the side and felt no obstacle, then reached back to find a corner of the marble wall. I assumed that I had now reached the junction where the three upstairs corridors joined together near the front of the building.

The light was definitely stronger before me and I could tell that it was coming from somewhere below the floor I was on. I then remembered that there was a central shaft, just off the front lobby, that extended from the first floor all the way up to the domed ceiling, high above the floor where I now stood.

Thoughts of rescue seemingly assured, I carefully inched my way forward until I could feel the circular railing that bounded the balcony around the shaft. Grasping that cold rail as though it alone could save me, I leaned over the waist high railing and looked down three stories to the main floor. The light was stronger at ground level, no doubt coming in from the main doors, but even so, I could make out objects below only dimly. I listened intently for some time, praying for the sound of voices or even footsteps, but I heard nothing.

I called out once again, hoping against hope for a reply from below. I had, however, forgotten how my voice could echo down these empty passageways and now, as I stood at the central junction of all three corridors, the resulting onslaught of echoes nearly froze my heart. The sound of my plaintive voice bounced off the domed ceiling and variegated walls, rolling down the corridors, reverberating over and over again, until it seemed I was surrounded by questioning voices. My heart pounding, I whirled around to face the darkness behind me, certain I would see some malevolent monster lunging at me, but there was nothing there and as the echoes slowly died away, I heard not another sound. With panic once more creeping over me, I realized that I was not going to be rescued—that I must now find my own way downstairs and then outside.

Breathing deeply several times to calm myself, I

seemed to vaguely recall that the stairs I had ascended earlier today had been somewhere to the left of the central shaft where I now stood. My eyes darting about as I tried vainly to penetrate the surrounding darkness, I moved slowly and quietly around the balcony, following the railing until I could just distinguish a somewhat darker square of blackness in the wall across from me. I hoped that this would prove to be the entryway to the staircase I so desperately sought.

It was with a great force of will that I left that spot of dim light and entered once again into the darkness, but I was becoming frantic to get myself out of this tomb. Hands outstretched before me, I moved slowly across the marble floor until I encountered a cold wall beneath my fingertips. Releasing the breath I had been unconsciously holding, I placed my left hand against the wall and started moving toward where I thought the stairwell should be. After traveling ten or twelve feet with only the solid wall beneath my hand, I feared that I must have somehow overshot the alcove and was just about to turn and retrace my steps when I felt the trace of a cool breeze against my face. If I had not been bathed in a faint sheen of perspiration at the time, I might not have noticed the change in the air as it moved past me. I took another step forward and discovered an unseen, absolutely black opening next to me.

I hesitated a moment, trying to collect my thoughts. This movement of air, the first I had noticed since leaving the flower room, informed me that a stairway must lie within the darkness near at hand—stairs that would lead me to freedom. Yet I still hesitated, not liking the analogy my mind had suddenly grasped upon of likening this dark portal to the waiting, open mouth of some unseen, unknown beast which was waiting only for me to step inside and then the mouth would snap shut, trapping me within its maw to eventually devour me.

Shaking off those thoughts as being just barely unreasonable, I glanced back for a final look at the dim glow of light emanating from the central shaft area. Then, taking a deep breath, I moved forward into the waiting darkness.

Here, I moved with even more caution, as I certainly did not want to go tumbling blindly down the unseen stairs somewhere before me. Placing one foot in front of the other and feeling about with the toe of my shoe before moving forward again, I had crept across about six feet of floor when my foot struck a metal object. Exploring the item with my hands, I deduced that it was a wrought iron guard rail and by further examination with my feet, I soon found the first step leading down into the fathomless darkness. My heart fairly leaped at the thought that I had finally found a possible means of escape.

There was, however, yet another slight problem. I was absolutely certain that the stairs I had climbed earlier in the day had been surmounted by a wooden banister, not one of wrought iron. I recalled this fact distinctly, as I had to clutch at the wooden railing rather desperately on several occasions during my ascent to the third floor, in order to steady myself.

TERRY D. SCHEERER

Regardless of the fact that these stairs were not the ones I had expected to find, they did lead down, which was the direction I needed to go. So, I decided to descend them and worry about finding the main doors when I had reached the ground floor. Grasping the cold metal handrail tightly with both hands, I started down, moving slowly and carefully.

After descending only a few steps, I had the uneasy feeling that the stairs seemed to be curving back in on themselves. A few steps more confirmed my suspicion; I was on a circular staircase and I was positive I had not seen it previously. Nevertheless, I continued my way blindly downward, for I knew I had no other option open to me.

I begin to count the successive stairs as I went, mainly to keep my mind from thinking about what might be lurking in the darkness around me, but I gave up the count after several more circuits of the stairwell. I kept picturing a crazed Vincent Price in the film "The Pit and the Pendulum", descending a circular stone staircase on his way to the torture chamber below his castle. At least he could see where he was going as he circled down to his doom—I was unable to see anything. I found myself listening intently for any furtive sounds of pursuit from above, or perhaps worse yet, the sound of someone (or something) waiting in the darkness below.

Continuing to descend, I felt that by now I must have traversed enough stairs to account for all three stories of the mausoleum, even with the backtracking due to the curvature of the staircase, yet they continued

48

downward. While I might have indeed passed by doorways leading onto other floors, totally unseen in the darkness, I thought that there would have at least been a noticeable landing on each successive floor. Not having many alternatives, however, I continued down until my thoughts were jarred as my foot came down unexpectedly short of the next stair. My heart pounding, I felt about with my foot for a moment and then nearly shouted with joy at the realization that I had at last reached a level area.

Waiting not even a moment to hold in check my mounting excitement, I blundered through the darkness before me, no longer concerned about unseen obstacles or even the possibility of a yawning emptiness of another stairwell—I simply had to find a way out of that suffocating blackness. Within only three short steps, I crashed headlong into a wooden barrier. Hoping against hope, I felt about frantically and discovered that it was, indeed, a door. My heart near to bursting with joy at finally finding an exit, my questing hands soon found the handle, but suddenly I hesitated. God forbid—what if the door was locked?

Forcing such defeatist thoughts from my feverish mind, I quickly attempted to turn the door handle and was immensely relieved when it rotated easily. I pulled on the handle, intending to fling wide the door on my route to freedom, but icy fingers gripped my heart. The door would not budge. I nearly cried aloud in anguish at that moment, my fear and frustration were so great. Choking back a sob of despair, I tried the door again and yet again, jerking at the handle so vigorously the door begin to rattle within its frame.

Quickly exhausted by my futile efforts to open that portal of freedom, I sagged to the floor and warm tears slid down my flushed cheeks. In utter defeat, I pounded weakly on the door with my fist and a gasp caught in my throat as the door swung silently outward into a dimly illuminated passageway.

It then seemed ridiculously obvious—in my initial excitement, I had been wasting my energy trying to pull at the door, while it was meant to open the other way. Cursing myself for ten different kinds of a fool, I heaved myself to my feet and peered through the doorway. Even the dim light that now greeted my eyes appeared blindingly strong since I had been so long in the darkness and it was several moments before I could readily focus on what was before me. Whatever I had been expecting to encounter, it was surely not the sight that now greeted me.

The wall across from the doorway appeared to be white marble and I noted that the ceiling seemed oppressively low. My eyes now growing accustomed to the light, I stepped into what turned out to be a long, seemingly empty corridor. Looking first to my right and then to my left, my breath seemed to catch in my throat and I staggered backwards to clutch at the door frame for support.

Fresh sweat broke out on my forehead, for all that the air around me held an uncomfortable chill. I realized with growing fright that I must now be even below the level of the outside street—I was now actually beneath the ground. Stretching away from me on either side, the passage appeared endless and there were words chiseled into the marble wall across from me and down both sides of the passageway. Names and dates were visible in the cold stone—dates of birth, as well as dates of death.

Now I hoped that I was truly dreaming, for I realized that by trying to escape that labyrinth of the dead from which I had awakened, I had unwittingly descended much too far and I was now in a gigantic underground crypt. My breath was coming in ragged gasps and the oppression I had felt earlier at being surrounded by the dead was now multiplied tenfold. Not only was I still surrounded by an untold number of rotting corpses, but now, above me were a full threes stories of the dead seemingly pressing me down into the ground. My entire body began to shake at the thought that I was trapped with thousands upon thousands of moldering bodies as my only companions in this nightmarish place.

The air, though cold, had a musty, ancient taste to it, as if undisturbed by the faintest movement of fresh air for millennia. Thoughts of Lovecraftian horror flooded my fevered brain as I strained my ears to catch the slightest sound from up and down that dimly lighted passage, the ends of which appeared to fade away in the misty haze in both directions. Only a chill silence assailed my senses, but even that did little to ease my growing fear.

Nearing panic, I turned back to the stairway, preparing to run back up the stairs, but the darkness therein halted me. Only a small amount of dim light entered the stairwell, illuminating but the first six feet of winding stairs and as I stared into the featureless darkness above me, I knew that I was not brave enough to leave even this meager light to once again enter that Stygian realm. At least in my present position I would be able to see my way as I moved about and I shuddered yet again at the prospect of once more fighting my way through that unknown blackness in an attempt to find an exit. I was obviously still lost, but I tried to calm myself, somewhat, with the hopeful assurance that there must be another way out of this crypt, other than the one I had used to gain entry.

Steeling myself as best I could and taking a deep breath, I moved out into the middle of the passage, wishing to keep as much distance as possible between myself and the marble enclosed tombs that lined the walls. One direction appearing as good as the other, I started off in a direction which I hoped would lead me to the front of the building, assuming the most likelihood of an ascending stairway lying in that area. The light—what there was of it—came from behind stone outcroppings near the low ceiling, but as I slowly traversed the passage, I noticed that in some areas the lights were dark. Whether that section of lights were burned out or were dark for some other reason, I could not know, but passing through those areas of shadow was extremely disheartening and I hurried my steps each time I approached one of those lightless sections.

I was soon disgusted to note that in many places where the floor met the walls, rather large, long-legged, pale spiders had spun asymmetrical webs, the silken strands sometimes reaching many inches up the wall. Here and there too, the wretched creatures themselves would occasionally scuttle jerkily across the floor in front of me as I continued down the passage. I wondered vaguely what might have sustained those vile life forms in this sunless, airless tomb, but whatever it may have been, I certainly did not want to run across any of them. I also noticed in several places long lines of thick, gray dust had piled up against the base of the walls, the entire effect seemingly one of if not total disuse, then at the very least, a long neglect of my surroundings. This visual information did nothing to ease my mind concerning a readily located egress from this place.

As I moved cautiously forward, my eyes were inevitably drawn to the chiseled features on the walls around me. When I saw some of the dates on the vaults near me, I slowed my progress and eventually stopped completely, fascination overcoming my fear. The dates of death that I read on those tombs all appeared surprisingly old: 1864, 1857, 1842, 1838. Apparently, all of the deceased which were entombed in this area had died well over one hundred years ago.

I was somewhat amazed by this discovery, as I knew that the mausoleum itself was only some sixty or seventy years old. I therefore theorized that the hundreds, perhaps thousands of bodies entombed in this underground vault must have been transported from their original resting places and re-entombed here, presumably sometime after the structure was first erected. Either that, or the present structure had been built over the top of the older crypt, one that had been on this location for over a hundred years. I could not know the answer to this question, but I could guess that there were surely no longer any relatives of these long dead souls to still mourn their passing or to bring flowers to their crypts. The obvious neglect of this place seemed to reinforce the idea that these dead were indeed long forgotten and perhaps totally ignored. This train of thought only tended to agitate my already fearful mind and I hurried on, trying not to look at any more of the dates carved into the walls.

As I quickly continued down the passage, I was startled to come upon a branching corridor and momentarily hope swelled within me. It was just as quickly dashed, however, as this new passageway appeared identical to the one I now traversed. It too seemed to stretch away endlessly, until the light appeared too dim to distinguish any further details. The total number of bodies actually entombed within this necropolis began to stagger my mind and I realized this damnable maze must honeycomb the entire under-surface of the mausoleum grounds.

Hastening on, despair was rapidly engulfing me once again and I thought my situation totally hopeless, when I noticed a change in the quality of light some way ahead of me. Having no better avenue to pursue, I trudged on, but did not get my hopes up at what I might find. The cold seemed to be slowly eating into my bones and I hugged my arms around my chest and began to quicken my steps—more to keep warm than

54

to hurry my progress.

I soon reached the area I had sighted previously and the light was indeed brighter here. I slowed my steps as I neared a low doorway, recessed into the wall on my left. It was from this doorway that a soft, warm light spilled into the passage. I then became aware of something that had been playing around the edges of my mind for some time. I stopped short of the doorway and listened intently.

Unmistakably, I could hear music.

I must have been subconsciously aware of it for some time, but the melody was so soft, so unlike anything I had ever heard before, I must have simply put it off as a trick my mind was playing on me, brought on by the long imposed silence I had suffered through the past hour, or so. And yet, the more I strained to catch that spectral tune, the more I came to realize that I was not actually hearing the music — rather, I seemed to feel the notes within my brain. The music was simply there, in my head.

While I knew that what I was experiencing was physically impossible, that fact did not seem to bother me as much as I thought it should. In point of fact, an unusual and unexpected sense of well being was seeping into my body, making my fears of just a few minutes ago now seem somehow far behind me. As I stood there, the music enveloped me with a gentle warmth and my sense of well being increased, while my fears dissolved away completely. Feeling a trifle lightheaded, but in a better frame of mind than I could remember processing for days, I stepped forward to

55

peer through the open doorway.

Three, well worn stone steps led down to a wide, low-ceilinged, empty room. I descended the steps and looked about at my surroundings. Directly across from the entrance was what appeared to be another, much larger doorway, but it was set horizontally to the floor, about halfway up the wall. I could think of nothing it could be used for and other than that peculiar item, the faded walls and floor of the room were bare.

And yet, this was definitely where the music I seemed to sense was coming from. It appeared to swell and ebb, all around me, never letting me quite catch hold of it. Entranced, I advanced to the center of the room and did a slow pirouette, taking in the entire, empty scene.

However, I was apparently wrong, for the room was not entirely empty, after all.

As I slowly turned, I found that I would catch fleeting glimpses of movement out of the corners of my eyes, but as I came to fully face the spot where the movement seemed to have been, there was nothing there. Yet it kept happening as I continued to turn 'round, the wraith-like glimpses slowly coalescing into vague, transparently human forms. I surprised myself by still feeling no fear at this new and totally unexpected development. The warmth I had felt within me earlier had increased and I was now completely at peace.

At last I stood still and faced one of the blank walls expectantly. A fine mist seemed to hover near the wall and as I watched, it slowly solidified and I smiled, even as tears of happiness edged up and over my lower lashes to spill softly against my cheeks.

Now I knew the reason for my gentle inner peace; for there, smiling back at me in that soft, reassuring way she had always used to banish all of my fears as a child, was my beloved grandmother. She was softly transparent, as I could still see the wall behind where she sat, but it was she, all the same. The how or wherefore of this most welcome sight did not enter my mind at all—it was enough that she was there with me, in my time of need, just as she had always been before.

I started toward her, wanting above all else to embrace her once again, but she held up her hand to stay me. Her lips did not move, but I heard her words as well as if they had been spoken aloud. She asked me not to mourn for her, as she was now at peace, surrounded by friends and it was this new found peace she wanted to share with me.

She explained how she had been aware of my presence in the tomb and of my fear and confusion. With the aid of her new friends, she had guided me to this room so that I might see her once more and have my fears and sorrow put to rest. This day being February 2nd (I had not realized how much time had passed, but it was now after midnight), the spirits celebrated, as they always did on this date and I was to be privileged to witness this annual fete.

Her words, or rather her thoughts and her very presence relieved my mind of much of its uncertainty. I knew that I would now be able to go on with my life without fear and with a glad heart, for her soul was truly at peace. Nodding to her through my tears of happiness, I could see she understood that I was now at peace, as well.

Still smiling, she gestured toward the room and I slowly tore my eyes from her to gaze about myself. My perception was slightly blurred from the tears and I wiped rather haphazardly at my eyes with the sleeve of my coat. Unnoticed by me for the few moments I had beheld my departed one, the music once again began to swell around and through me and I was only mildly surprised to discover that the once apparently empty room was now filed with ghost like shapes, mostly paired off and dancing around the room in time to the hypnotic melody which seemed to fill the air.

Some of the specters appeared more substantial than others, but from all of them there exuded a sense of peace and contentment. Young and old there were and from what I could tell, the fashions represented everything from present day dress, to the style of attire worn during the civil war. I was enchanted by the whole scene and watched fascinated as the spirits danced around me, apparently oblivious to my presence. Their movements were so graceful and totally unencumbered, they seemed to float across the floor, yet I could see their feet making contact beneath them.

Full of awe, I turned back to my grandmother and saw her in apparent conversation with the apparition of a young girl, perhaps no more than eighteen years of age—at least when she had died. They both looked my way and the girl smiled shyly as she briefly met my curious gaze. With an encouraging nod from my grandmother, the girl glided slowly over to where I was standing.

She stopped a few feet away from me, her white gloved hands clasped before her and her eyes demurely lowered. She was quite short and rather thin, her dark hair swept up from her neck in an elaborate bun and her long dress was reminiscent of the styles worn in the early 1900s. She raised her eyes to me and I could see that she was quite pretty and I felt a sudden stab of sorrow that she should have died at so young an age.

As I gazed down at her, I felt the gentle urging of my grandmother in my mind and I smiled at the sweet ghost before me. Knowing it was what my dear grandmother wished, I bowed slightly from the waist and held out my hands to the vision in front of me. She came forward and placed her gloved hand in mine—it felt as though I held a feather in my palm. Her other hand she placed softly on my right shoulder. So light was her touch, I could not even be sure her hand was actually resting there. I slipped my arm around her slim waist, my hand meeting only the slightest resistance as I touched her. Then gazing into each other's eyes, we joined the other dancers.

I had rarely danced previous to that moment and I surely could not have known how to keep in step to that completely unearthly music, but we twirled around the room as if I had done so every day of my life. There was no misstep, no faltering movements on my part and surely none on hers. We glided about as if we were one entity and I did not even consider how such miracles were possible. My heart soared and my soul with it, until I too seemed to be floating several inches off the floor.

As we swept past the place my grandmother was seated, I turned to look over at her and her smile filled me with such love and such warm happiness, I knew my mourning for her was no longer necessary. She was now truly at peace and she only wanted the same thing for me. I smiled back at her, without tears this time and she knew that I understood her feelings and would, from here on, be all right.

I continued to dance, all trace of fatigue gone from me and returned my attention to my partner. She seemed so fragile, so light in my arms that I dared not breath too hard, for fear I might inadvertently blow her image away. She must have sensed what I had been thinking, for she smiled up at me, full of youthful innocence and gaiety.

We danced on for what seemed like hours, yet I felt I could have continued in the same vein, forever. It was not to be, however, for I suddenly found myself alone in the middle of the room, the music I had been dancing to now only a dim memory. The apparitions had likewise vanished, as smoke is dispelled by a gentle breeze. Of a sudden, I was extremely exhausted and I barely managed to stumble over to the nearest wall where I fairly collapsed onto the floor.

Sleep was rapidly overtaking me and the last thing I can recall is the voice of my grandmother, coming to me faintly, as if from a great distance, telling me never to forget her love for me and to remember the peace and happiness of this night. Then, she reassured me, just before I fell into a deep sleep, as she had done every night for so many years while I was a child, not to fear; her spirit would always be close to me and everything would ultimately be all right as long as I had faith in myself. As I drifted off, I thought I felt a soft flutter against my cheek, as if a pair of lips had gently brushed my face. I never knew whether that last touch was from my grandmother, or from my ghostly dancing partner. It didn't really matter. I would have liked to think it had been from both of them, wishing me goodbye, together.

# # #

I was awakened some time later by the sound of strange voices and once I had squeezed the sleep from my eyes, I realized the voices were coming from the passageway beyond. I staggered to my feet, my entire body feeling unaccountably stiff and sore—no doubt from sleeping in a cramped position on the cold, hard floor—and lurched over to the doorway. A few feet down the passage, two men were carrying on an animated conversation, their backs to me. I hailed them with undisguised relief and needless to say, they were quite surprised to find me there.

At first they were somewhat belligerent toward me. They must have thought I was a burglar, it being so early in the morning and the mausoleum not yet open to the public, but what on earth could I possibly have stolen in such a place? After I had related my story to them and they viewed my appearance, they became very helpful and even apologetic about my adventure. They led me upstairs—I could hardly believe it, but the stairway to the ground floor was but a dozen feet beyond the room in which I had spent most of the night—and took me directly to the manager's office.

It turned out to be after eight o'clock in the morning and while one of the workmen went in to explain my unusual circumstances to the manager, I waited in the reception area. I was treated to a welcome cup of coffee by a quietly efficient secretary, who kept stealing curious glances at me whenever she thought I wasn't looking her way.

Very quickly, the manager appeared, nearly fawning over me in his attempt to sooth and placate me. Mr. Gilstrap, as his name turned out to be, must have thought that I was intent upon suing the establishment for negligence at my having been locked within the mausoleum overnight. I assured him that I harbored no ill feelings toward either him or the owners and proceeded to make an explanation as to what had befallen me.

Before I could begin, however, he ushered me into his office and had me seated on a couch so I could tell my story in a more relaxed vein. I then told him of my waking in the flower room and of my subsequent mistaken descent into the subterranean vault, where, after wandering about for some time without being able to find an exit, I had apparently collapsed in the room where I was found and had obviously slept until

I was awakened by the workmen. I did not bother relating to him the curious dream I had (for dream it surely must have been) while sleeping in that dusty, empty room—of seeing and speaking to my deceased grandmother and dancing the night away with the apparition of a long dead, young woman.

He repeatedly apologized for my misfortunes and seemed much relieved that I chose to be so magnanimous about the whole affair. He then offered me the use of his private washroom to freshen myself up a bit. I had not even noticed my appearance in the excitement of being rescued, but now I took stock of myself and discovered that I certainly did look quite disheveled. My suit was terribly wrinkled and dust, grime and not a few cobwebs stained my clothes. With a sigh, I gratefully accepted his offer to set myself presentable, once again.

Stepping into the washroom, I was rather shocked by the vision I presented to myself in the mirror. My hair was badly tousled and I had telltale streaks on my face where tears had left faint tracks in the dust and grime. I quickly brushed at my hair with my fingers, washed my face and hands and set about dusting myself off. As I brushed at the sleeves of my jacket, I caught sight of something in the mirror that froze my movements and brought back sharply the events of the supposed dream I had experienced during the night. I slowly bent near the mirror to examine myself more closely and finally realized with a surge of happiness that what had happened last night had not been a dream, after all.

I silently sent out my love and thanks to both my dear grandmother and to my lovely dance partner of the night before. I now knew that my 'dream' had been real; that I had actually seen and spoken to my grandmother's spirit, as well as witnessed all of those other apparitions as they danced through the night. For there, on my right shoulder, in the exact spot where my partner had rested her palm while we danced, was the unmistakable, dusty imprint of a small and delicate hand.

The End

Death Chant

I have worked in the medical field for nearly twenty years, off and on, and I realized a few years ago that I had never written a story dealing with the medical profession. So, the idea for this story came to me one night while at work—in a hospital—and since more horrific, frightening and terrible incidents occur in hospitals than in other service industry (aside from Government controlled services) , I felt obligated to share one such incident with the public. It was only a coincidence that shortly after this story was completed, the person whom I used as a basis for the main character just happened to disappear from the hospital. Honest.

Regardless, if on some quiet night, you are wandering the darkened hallways of a local hospital, be prepared to quickly turn around and head the other direction if you hear from behind a closed door, the soft murmurings of a...

Death Chant

AT 11:24, THE PM shift charge nurse was just finishing up her report to the night crew. Laurie, the night charge, was making out the shift assignments as Shirley added, almost as an afterthought, "Oh, and the old lady in room 250 passed about 9:30."

Laurie looked up from her paperwork. "That was Mrs. Enderlander," she said and sighed. "She was such a nice old lady. A shame we couldn't do more to help her."

Shirley rose and stretched, then gathered up her purse and coat. "Well, she had been here for days and had been sick for quite a while. We all have to go sometime, you know," she said with a shrug of her shoulders.

"How old was she, anyway? 92 or something?"

"Her chart says she was 94."

"Wow. I should live so long," Laurie said with a slight smile. "Has she been picked up yet?"

"No. Her son has been in there all evening and wanted some time alone with her before they came for the body. We didn't need the room right away, so I told him to take as much time as he needs." She slipped on her coat and slung her purse over one shoulder. "See you guys tomorrow night."

Laurie gave a wave as Shirley left the station and then went back to passing out the room assignments.

# # #

At about ten minutes to midnight, Angela approached room 250. A twenty-year-old nursing student, she was working her way through school and picking up much needed experience by working the night shift as a CNA. Angela had been on duty the last few nights, so knew both Mrs. Enderlander and her son. She had come to like the sweet old lady, but still wasn't sure how she felt about the son. He was a small, quiet old guy—must have been in his middle to late seventies— and seemed harmless enough, but there was just something about him that gave her the creeps.

Oh, well, Laurie had said that he was still sitting with his mother and since this was one of her rooms tonight, Angela had to go in and check on him. She had seen a lot of dead bodies during her eighteen months as a CNA, but she had never gotten used to being around them. Maybe it was just as well that Mr. Enderlander was still here. She took a deep breath, tapped lightly on the door and pushed it open.

Angela slowly entered the darkened room and stopped just inside the doorway. The window curtains had been pulled shut, so the only illumination came from a single bulb over the sink in the bathroom, next to where she now stood. Some light spilled into the room from the hallway, but as the door slowly closed behind her, even that small comfort was taken away. Near the window, Angela could see Mrs. Enderlander's bed; the body covered with a sheet that was pulled up to her chin, leaving only her small head exposed.

In the dim light, Angela could not make out any details of the woman's face, which was probably just as well. In a chair next to the head of the bed, Mr. Enderlander sat with his back toward Angela. He apparently had not heard her enter the room, as he was hunched over, rocking gently back and forth and mumbling to himself. In one hand he held a small black box, which he was shaking—first toward the bed, then up in the air over his head, repeating these motions, over and over again. Something inside the box rattled, softly.

She stood there for a few moments, still and quiet, not wanting to disturb the old man or whatever bizarre ritual he might be performing. When he suddenly spoke, the sound made her jump. "Good evening, Angela," he said, softly, without turning around.

"Um... hi, Mr. Enderlander," she replied, rubbing the back of her neck where for some reason the short hairs had just stood straight up. Taking another deep breath, she took one more step into the room. "I was

69

really sorry to hear about your mother."

"Thank you, Angela," he said, still without turning to face her. "My mother thought quite highly of you."

"Really?" she asked, a slight smile touching her lips as she moved a bit farther into the room.

"Oh, yes. She looked forward to seeing you every night."

"Well. That's really nice. I was glad to be able to help her, you know."

"We both appreciated your dedication, my dear," he told her, his voice soft and soothing.

Angela wrung her hands together for a moment, not knowing how else she could help the old man. "Um… is there anything I can do for you, Mr. Enderlander?"

Turning in his chair to finally face her, he asked quietly, "I know that you are busy, my dear, but would it be a terrible imposition for you to perhaps sit with me for just a short while?"

Angela glanced at her watch and then looked a bit nervously at the closed door behind her, unsure if she wanted to be alone with this man, not to mention the fact that the room also contained a dead body. But when she turned back to Mr. Enderlander, she saw only a tired old man who had just lost his mother, someone who had been the center of his world for the past seventy years. Angela couldn't imagine a relationship ever lasting that long and decided that after such a loss, she could be a kind enough person to give him a few minutes of her precious time. "Sure, I can stay a while," she told him and flashed a brief smile. "I've finished my rounds and have a few minutes to myself."

The old man's face brightened considerably at her words. "Thank you, Angela," he said, softly. "Your company will do me a world of good, right now."

"Oh, that's all right," she told him, moving over to stand near the foot of the bed. "I really did like your mom. Even though she was real sick, she was always kind to me—never demanding, like some older patients are when they're in the hospital."

"Yes, well, that was her way," he said and turned to gaze at his mother's face.

They were quiet for some time and Angela noticed the black box he still held. "So, what were you doing when I came in?" she asked. "If I'm not prying, that is."

"Hmm? Oh, not at all," he told her and held the box up so the dim light reflected off the smooth, dull surface. "In our culture, the spirit of a departed loved one must be guided to the next world by someone who is still living. That honor usually falls to the next of kin, although, sometimes, the deceased chooses someone with the tribal shaman's powers to be the guide."

Confused, but intrigued, Angela asked, "What culture would that be?"

"Ah," he said, turning his eyes toward her with what now seemed to glow in the weak light that was coming from behind her. "My people came originally from Eastern Europe—from places long since forgotten by history, I'm afraid. We can, however, with accuracy, trace our family line back over two thousand years, to a time of great warrior kings and pagan seers, when men shared with their people the knowledge of nature and how to live in harmony with Her. We were transplanted from our homes many generations ago, of course, but my family was a powerful force in the known world before the Romans invaded our lands and attempted to exterminate our beliefs and my people.

"We persevered, however," he continued, a thin smile cutting across his lined face. "Our numbers were severely reduced by countless wars and were further scattered by time, but there are still some of us left who follow the old ways."

Angela was not at all sure what he was talking about and put off his ramblings to grief and exhaustion. "So, you were trying to guide your mother's spirit somewhere special when I came into the room," she stated. At least she was fairly sure about that much of his story. "I didn't interrupt anything, did I?"

His smile became a sad line now, turning down the corners of his mouth and his eyes returned to their normal, dull shine. "No, my dear. Our little trance did not affect my attempt to guide my mother's spirit." He sighed before continuing. "My mother was a strong-willed woman and she was not ready to leave this world, even though she knew that her time here was over. So, her spirit is most likely still in this plane of existence and it is now seeking my attempt at guidance."

Still not sure exactly what was going on, but more curious than ever, Angela asked, "So, is that why she might stay…well…here, a while longer?"

Enderlander nodded. "It could, but the longer a spirit stays on this plane, without guidance, the more difficult it becomes to travel over. Eventually it might become lost, forgetting the reason for its existence and would wander, possibly forever, seeking a reason for its loss and sorrow; something that could never be found on its own."

"You mean, like a ghost?"

"Indeed," he replied. "And I do not wish my mother's spirit to undergo such a fate. Unfortunately, I am old and tired and apparently my own weakened spirit is not strong enough to help her make the transition."

"Gee. Is there anything I can do to help?" she asked with genuine concern.

"Ah, well," he said, the gleam returning to his eyes. "Actually, it is sometimes much easier for a younger spirit to guide a departed one, than say, an older, tired spirit like my own."

"Really?" Angela was still very curious about this whole concept of spirits moving from one plane to another. She didn't understand much of what the old man was saying, but she knew that she wanted to help him.

"Indeed," Enderlander said, softly, his thin smile slowly returning.

Angela took a couple of steps closer to the old man. "What can I do?"

He opened his palm, showing the small cube, once again. A soft, muffled rattle could be heard within the box.

73

She moved in a bit closer, her eyes on the box. "You were shaking that when I came in," she said quietly. "What's it for?"

Enderlander moved the box to within inches of her face, and then gently took hold of her hand. "With this," he replied softly, so softly, it was almost a breath, as he leaned in toward her, "with this, we seek a guide to accept the soul of the departed spirit, to guide it into the next life."

Smiling, Enderlander pressed the bottom of the dark cube with his thumb and a hole formed on top of the box. Small at first, the hole grew slowly larger, until it seemed to be bigger than the box, itself. "Look into the box, my dear," he told her, his voice soothing and slick.

Angela gazed into the dark hole that now appeared to be nearly the size of her head and was suddenly frightened. She tried to pull back, but Enderlander held tight to her wrist. Eyes still locked on the growing darkness before her, Angela whimpered in terror, but found that she was unable to move. Down in the depths of that black void something was slowly swirling, drawing her gaze ever deeper into the darkness.

"Join the others, my dear," the old man whispered, his words somehow calming her fears. "Do you hear them calling?" Angela did hear what she thought were voices calling her name, but very faintly, as if they were far, far away. "They are calling you, my child. They need you. I need you. We all need you," he hissed in her ear.

Angela weakly nodded her head, her eyelids now so heavy she could barely keep them open. From a distance, she could hear the old man chanting again, his voice rising and falling in concert with the beating of her heart. No longer aware of anything save the rhythmic sound of the chant and the intense urge to help this kind, gentle man, she looked deeper and deeper into the yawning opening. A sense of vertigo swept over her as she leaned toward the now huge hole and she felt something like cold hands reaching out of the swirling darkness, taking hold of her wrists, drawing her gently down... deeper... ever deeper...

# # #

At twenty-three minutes after midnight, Laurie knocked lightly on the door of room 250 and then pushed it open, almost bumping into Mr. Enderlander. "Oh, I'm so sorry," she said, backing up a step. "I wasn't sure if you were still here."

"That is quite all right," he told her. "I was in fact, just leaving."

"Is everything all right, then?" she asked, looking past him into the room where his mother lay on the bed, a sheet drawn up to her neck.

Following her gaze, Enderlander smiled. "Yes. My mother's spirit is at rest and everything is finally as it should be." He turned back to face her. "I would like to extend my most sincere thanks for all of your kindness and assistance during my mother's stay." He held out his hand and Laurie took it, surprised at his sincerity.

75

She shook his hand gently, since he did not make any attempt to squeeze her own—it was more a caress on his part than a handshake and she quickly released her grip.

"Not at all, Mr. Enderlander," Laurie told him, feeling the need to wipe her hand off, as soon as possible. "Your mother was a kind woman and seemed very sweet."

"Ah, yes. She had her moments," he said, nodding his head, slightly and smiling up at her. "But, thank you, once again."

"Of course." Laurie backed up so he could get clear of the room. "Everything is arranged, so you just go on home and get some rest, now."

"Yes. Yes, indeed I will." He had a coat draped over one arm and a small cloth bag in his hand. Laurie thought she heard a soft rattle from inside the bag as he moved past her. "Good night, then," he said and headed for the elevators.

Laurie nodded and stepped into the room, but then turned back. "Excuse me, Mr. Enderlander, but have you seen Angela, tonight, by any chance?"

The old man slowly turned around and looked her right in the eyes. "Sorry, no," he said. "I haven't seen her tonight."

"Oh, well, it's no problem. She may just be in another room, helping someone."

"Yes, I suppose. Well, if you see her, be sure to share with her my heartfelt thanks and appreciation for all she did to help my mother and myself."

"Of course," Laurie assured him. The old man gave

her a tired wave and then walked slowly down the hall.

Shaking her head, Laurie turned on the overhead light in the room and moved over next to the bed. She reached down and pulled the sheet up over the body's face and then thought, 'How odd that Mr. Enderlander would say to thank Angela *if* I saw her tonight, rather than when I saw her. Almost as if he didn't expect me to ever see her again...'

Between the Moon and Mars

The title of this story may confuse some who read it, because it is not a science fiction story, nor does it take place in space (although the consequences of the story were determined by a space voyage) . I wrote this some time ago, no doubt because I grow increasingly tired and frustrated with the human race and its actions, its ignorance and its selfishness. This story is fiction, but that does not mean it could not happen, someday. So, be prepared if a neighbor comes knocking on your door, asking you to join him for a barbecue some warm summer day in the not too distant future.

Especially if he starts talking about a journey...

Between the Moon and Mars

SOMETIME IN THE not too distant future —

Carter Hartley, CEO of the largest pharmaceutical research company on the West Coast, skimmed over the last page of the electronic report and tossed the data pad onto his desk. The pad slid across the polished, antique rosewood and came to a stop scant inches from the far edge of the huge desk. "I don't see how they can blame us for any of this," he said to the other man in his office.

Hudson Clark stood silently, lost in thought with his back to the desk, gazing out of the floor-to-ceiling windows at the city, sixty-two floors below him. When he finally spoke, it was softly, as if he were speaking only to himself. "Do you know how many people in this world could care less about our petty problems?"

81

"What?" Carter asked, not understanding how that question pertained

to the report.

"Damn near all of them," Hudson replied, still speaking softly. "And yet, do you have any idea how many people on this planet are going to become frantic to be involved with this project when the results of that report becomes widely known?" he asked. "Damn near all of them," Hudson answered his own question after a short pause.

Carter sighed, but didn't say anything else. He was used to his friend and partner's peculiar mood swings and had found that if he just ignored Clark's unusual verbal meanderings, he would eventually come back down to earth.

True to form, after a few more minutes of silent contemplation, Hudson turned from the window and moved over to plop his lanky frame down in one of the heavily upholstered chairs that faced the desk. "You missed the whole point of the report, Carter," he began, as if no time had passed since Hartley finished reading the contents of the data pad.

"Explain it to me."

Now it was Clarke's turn to sigh. "You've heard of California's giant redwoods, haven't you?" he asked from behind his long, steepled fingers.

"Of course I've heard of them," Carter answered. Though his offices were only a few hours from the very trees Hudson was talking about, Hartley had never taken the time to visit the forest of huge, ancient trees. His business had always kept him too busy to take time off for any sort of vacation, let alone one that would take him away from the creature comforts he had become so used to. "What about them?"

Clarke sighed, again. Deeply. "It was in the report, Carter," he said, trying not to sound too exasperated. "Some of those trees live to be over two thousand years old." Carter seemed unimpressed with this statistic, so Hudson continued. "About twenty-five years ago, a geneticist here in Northern California discovered a gene in the Sequoias that seemed to slow down cell degeneration. It appeared it was this gene that helped the trees live as long as they do."

Now Hudson detected a gleam in Carter's eye. He must have realized that there might be some way to make a profit from this information, but Clarke plowed ahead with his story before his partner could sidetrack him.

"While that discovery was considered a breakthrough in some scientific circles, nothing was done with it at the time and after a while it was just filed away and essentially forgotten about. That is, until some fifteen years ago when the Manned Mars Mission was in the early planning stages." He leaned forward in his chair and continued his lecture. "One of the many problems facing the Triple M project was how to store enough water, food and oxygen for two or perhaps three astronauts on board a craft that would also have to carry scientific gear and enough fuel to get them safely to Mars and then, of course, back home again on a journey that would last some sixteen to twenty months."

TERRY D. SCHEERER

Unable to sit still, Hudson got up and began to pace up and down, but was drawn back to the huge windows that formed two walls of Carter's office. He stared down from his lofty position at the teeming millions of people below as he continued speaking. "They had obtained some insight from past experiences with the Mir Space Station, as well as the International Space Station, such as how to recycle both air and water, but the Triple M project had its own set of problems. If the astronauts were to run short of supplies a hundred million miles from Earth, there wasn't going to be much anyone could do to help them. Of course, they were going to try and produce some of their own food during the trip—using a system of hydroponics—so the processed food they carried would only be used as a supplement, hopefully, but even so, two years is a long time for food to just sit around in a plastic tube and remain edible."

He turned back to face Carter before going on, "Then, one of the scientists on the project came across the research done on the Sequoia gene. He found if that gene was introduced into the cells of the processed foodstuffs, it slowed the breakdown of the cells, essentially keeping the food from spoiling for months, without the necessity for added preservatives or refrigeration." Carter didn't seem overly impressed by this breakthrough and Hudson moved over to put his hands on the desk and leaned toward the man.

"That meant they could stock the Triple M ship with more than enough food for the extended trip and didn't have to worry about any of it going bad before

84

they returned to Earth."

"I understand that part of it," Carter said, with a wave of his hand, "but how did we become involved with the Mars mission?"

"We didn't," Hudson replied, moving away from the desk and back to the window. "We became involved after they returned," he said, speaking softly, once again. "Something happened on that long trip to Mars, something that no one has yet been able to understand."

He became silent and Carter waited for him to continue. When he didn't speak for some time, Hartley finally asked, "So, what happened?"

Shaking off his inner thoughts, Hudson went on. "We know what happened, we just don't know why. Somewhere out there in the blackness of space between the moon and Mars the Sequoia gene changed. It mutated, for lack of a better term. It may have been the extended lack of gravity or perhaps it was cosmic radiation—nobody knows for sure, and why it happened isn't really that important. What is important is the result of that mutation." He turned back to face Carter, but didn't leave his place near the window.

"When the mutated gene was ingested and digested by the astronauts, it managed to attach itself to cells in their own bodies and then did the same thing to their cells as it did to the food cells. It slowed down cell deterioration."

Not sure if his friend meant to imply that this was good or bad, Carter had to ask, "Is that a good or bad result?"

Hudson sighed, again. "It depends on how you view the future of the human race," he answered, which didn't help Carter to understand the situation any better, at all.

"And that means...?" he prompted.

Turning back to the window, Hudson said, "Cells in the human body die all the time, but they are usually replaced with new cells, as the older cells die off. As the body ages, however, fewer new cells are produced and over the years as more cells die without being replaced, we inevitably age more rapidly. The eyesight goes, the hearing goes, muscle and bone weaken and deteriorate, all because cells die and aren't replaced." He moved back to stand in front of the desk to emphasize his next words.

For the most part during the past hundred and fifty years, the average life span has been slowly but steadily increasing. At one point, it was up to 87.6 years. That was the number of years the average human in Western society could expect to live. Unfortunately, in the past couple of decades, that average has declined rather drastically." He paused to wearily rub a hand over his face, before continuing. "Due to excessive air pollution, pesticides in our food, carcinogens in our water, strains of bacteria that have become immune to most known antibiotics and other, as yet undetermined reasons, the average life expectancy in the western world has now dropped to approximately 78.3 years and by all accounts is still on the decline.

"That is a huge drop in only twenty years," he

admitted, "and has frightened global scientists, who don't know if they can reverse this downward progression." Suddenly tired and frustrated, Hudson dropped himself back down into the chair and stared at his hands for a moment before continuing.

"Now, just imagine," he said, speaking softly once more, "if there was something that would slow down cell deterioration in the human body—something that would essentially slow the aging process and literally add decades to the normal life span—how much would that be worth to people?" he asked, looking up at Carter. "And what would people be willing to do to achieve this miracle?"

Carter slowly began to understand the implications of what Hudson was saying. "We have access to this, this gene?" he asked, his voice almost a whisper.

"In a manner of speaking, we do," Hudson admitted, although he didn't sound very happy about it. He leaned back in his chair and looked up at the ceiling. "When the astronauts returned from Mars, it was months before it was discovered that they weren't aging in a normal fashion and it was months more before anyone figured out what had caused the change. It was all top secret, of course. No one wanted to admit the possibility of a life-extending breakthrough until it had been sufficiently tested. That's where we came into the picture."

He leaned forward and placed his elbows on his knees, now staring at the floor. "We did experiments for almost two years, using what little of the food was brought back from the Mars mission. It turned out that we couldn't duplicate the gene mutation effect here on Earth. Whatever it was that happened to it could only take place out there," and he waved his hand toward the window, indicating the vastness of space.

"We fed some of the remaining food supply from the mission to animals and some to human volunteers. It worked the same on either species—cell deterioration was slowed, as was the aging process. But, we couldn't duplicate the gene mutation," he said, then slammed his fist down on the arm of his chair and got up, to begin pacing the room once again.

"Eventually, we put down the animals that had been affected by the mutant gene and fed that meat to additional volunteers." He stopped his pacing and wiped a shaky hand over his face. "It seems that the mutated gene can only be transferred from one cell group to another by the act of ingestion and digestion. Those volunteers who digested the mutated gene in the affected animal meat also exhibited a slowdown in cell deterioration."

"They actually stopped aging?" Carter asked.

"No, they didn't stop aging," Hudson assured him, "but they showed a definite slowing of the aging process. We won't know for decades how many years may have been added to their lives. There are too many variables—their age at the time of ingestion, their health at that time, other variables we haven't even worked out yet."

"So, the experiments are ongoing, then?" Carter asked, finally becoming excited at the possibilities of this breakthrough.

Hudson collapsed back into the chair and covered his face with his hands. "Only in the sense that we can follow the remaining volunteers," he admitted.

"What do you mean, 'the remaining volunteers'?" Carter asked, suddenly feeling a sinking sensation in his stomach. "How many are there?"

"We now have contact with eight of the original twenty-six volunteers."

"Eight?" Carter echoed. "What happened to the rest of them?" he asked, hoping he wasn't going to be told that they had somehow died as a result of the experiments.

"They walked away from the research complex in Delano two nights ago and basically disappeared," Clarke told him, his voice barely above a whisper.

Flabbergasted by this revelation, Carter demanded, "How was that allowed to happen?"

Hudson sprang from the chair and glared at his friend. "Christ, Carter, they weren't prisoners," he nearly shouted. "They were volunteers," he said, calming somewhat. "And they were apparently frightened when they discovered what was happening to them."

"Why would they be frightened?" Carter asked, almost shouting, himself. "They should have been thrilled to death at the prospect of living an extended life. Isn't that what everyone wants for themselves?"

"Of course it is. That's exactly why they were frightened."

Confused, Carter asked more calmly, "Explain that line of reasoning to me."

Hudson sighed and moved back over to the window and stared down at the city, knowing that somewhere out there, eighteen frightened people were living on borrowed time. He sighed, again. "The only way the mutant gene can be transferred to another living organism is by ingestion and the only samples of that gene we have left in the whole world are in the living tissue of those twenty-six volunteers." He turned and looked at Carter, who was slowly beginning to realize what Hudson was getting at. "What do you think the rest of Earth's population is going to do when they find out that only twenty-six people in the entire world have the potential to extend their lives by twenty, thirty, even fifty years or more?"

After a pause, Carter asked quietly, "But, no one knows about this, outside the company. Do they?"

"They didn't up until two nights ago," Hudson told him. "But now that the cat's out of the bag, so to speak, we aren't going to be able to keep this under wraps for very long." He turned back to the window. "Someone is going to be upset that he or she can't have this miracle for themselves and they will sound the alarm. They will tell other people that there are a few special humans who have something that the rest of us can not have. People will become jealous at first, then they will become angry and then they will attempt to seek out these special people and try to take from them that which they themselves do not have." He sighed, again. "It is, after all, only human nature to hate and then to destroy that which we do not understand, that which we want, but can not have."

Disturbed by the thought that his friend might actually be correct in his judgment of human behavior, Carter asked softly. "You're being just a bit hard on the human race, don't you think?"

Hudson slowly shook his head, but didn't answer. He continued staring out the window as a single tear welled up and over his eyelashes, dropping unnoticed to his cheek.

Less than a week later, the news that a life-extending gene had been discovered was known worldwide. When it was found out that the limited supply of this gene was being hoarded by only a handful of people, riots broke out. All over the world, frantic, angry people stormed the university and genetic research centers and frequently burned them to the ground when no information could be found on how to obtain this elusive gene. The "Gene" and the people who had it were now not only the talk of the town, but of the entire world.

A small talk radio station in Central California was no exception.

"Good evening, everyone. This is Tommy T. Martin, at *KILR*, that's *Killer Talk Radio*, your late night companion with a very special guest for your enjoyment tonight," Martin told his listening audience. "Tonight, we are privileged to bring you an interview with one of the most sought after people in the world. That's right, friends, tonight we have with us one of the original 'Gene' volunteers from the Delano research facility, right here in California." He waved his guest in toward the microphone on the other side of the console.

"Now, we promised our guest anonymity tonight," Martin said, checking the dials on his console and turning on the guest mike, "so I'll just call him Mr. G." He looked up at his guest and waited for him to nod his acceptance of that gesture.

"Welcome to Killer Talk Radio, Mr. G."

"Uh, well, thank you, Mr. Martin," the guest responded, nervously, leaning in toward the microphone as he spoke.

Martin waved him back, tapping at his headphones and shaking his head, indicating that he was too close to the mike. "Now, now, my friends just call me Tommy T, Mr. G," Martin told him, smiling at the rhyme he had made.

"Oh, well, all right," Mr. G said, tempted to lean in toward the mike, once again.

"Mr. G, our audience is anxious to know how you feel about carrying around this gene that is going to prolong your life."

"Well, Tommy," he started, but seeing Martin wave his hand in a circular, keep going kind of motion, added, "uh, well, Tommy T, when I first volunteered for this project, I certainly didn't have any idea that this was going to be happening to me."

"But, don't you feel it's unfair for you and only a few other people to have the benefit of this life extending gene, when there are so many millions of people in the world who would like to have access to it?"

"Well, sure, I guess to most people it might seem a bit unfair, at least at this point, but hopefully, somewhere down the road, I'm sure that this gene will be available to everyone."

"How can it be made available to everyone, if the only samples of it are held by you and a few other people?" Martin asked and Mr. G could sense a growing hostility coming from the man seated across from him.

"True, only a few people have the gene, now, but eventually scientists will be able to mass produce it. They're working around the clock on a solution to this problem, you know."

"Oh, sure," Martin snapped. "A solution, which if ever found, may be decades away and in the meantime, millions of people will grow older and die, while you don't age more than a few months. Do you really think that's fair, Mr. G?"

Becoming increasingly uncomfortable, he replied, "Now, look, Mr.

Martin, I didn't come here tonight to be attacked like this. It isn't my fault that I happen to accidentally have been given something you don't have access to. While I may understand your feelings of anger and frustration, there's nothing I can do to make things any different for you."

Martin smiled and said, "Oh, but there is something you can do to

make things different for me, Mr. G."

His guest heard an unexpected noise behind him

93

and turned to look over his shoulder. Through the large window that separated the control room from the room in which he was seated, he saw a dozen men, women and even children staring silently at him through the glass with haunted, hungry eyes. He whirled back to face Martin, suddenly very afraid.

"What is this, Martin?" he asked, his voice shaking. "You promised me this program was going to be taped and nobody outside of this room would ever know that I was going to be here tonight."

"That's right, Mr. G," Martin sneered, as he removed his headphones and slowly stood up. "My friends and I will make sure that no one outside of this room ever knows you were here."

As Martin started toward him around the console, Mr. G saw that the radio talk-jock now held a large butcher knife in one hand. But, as he heard the door open behind him and the sound of many feet shuffling into the room, what made him finally start screaming was the fact that in his other hand, Martin held a fork.

-

The Very Idea

This story was born from that famous question all writers are asked—

"Where do you get the ideas for all those stories you write?" I have often been asked that question myself, but will never give a truthful answer, because they would surely come after me if I told the truth. Who are "they" you ask? Well, after you read this story, you will have your answer to that question, as well as the answer to the one mentioned above. Beyond that explanation, you will have to come up with your own ideas and perhaps even discover to your utter horror…

-

The Very Idea

"I WANT TO thank you for coming on such short notice, Miss Wentworth," the old man said, as the reporter turned on a small tape recorder and sat down across from him.

"Well, I must admit that I was a bit surprised when you called, Mr.—"

"Please," he cut in, quickly. "No names on tape, as I stipulated."

"Oh, of course. I'm sorry." She crossed her legs, adjusting the hem of her skirt over her knees and placed the recorder on the coffee table. "As I was saying, I was surprised when you called to set up this interview. You haven't spoken to the press in nearly twenty years, isn't that correct?"

"Yes, yes, it has been quite some time, but I felt that I now needed to speak out regarding something that no one outside a select circle of people knows anything about."

"And what is that, sir?"

He leaned forward, his elbows resting on the arms of his wheelchair and spoke softly. "What is the one question asked of writers, more than any other question they might hear, no matter how long they have been writing?"

She thought about it for a moment, then admitted, "Well, I'm sure I don't know."

He gave a wicked little smile and said, "Where do you get the ideas for all those stories you write? That's it," he told her, spreading his thin arms wide and leaning back in his chair. "If I've heard that question once, I've heard it a thousand times and so has every other writer I've ever known."

Miss Wentworth smiled back at him. "Yes, I suppose many people who do not write would be curious about that."

"Of course they would. And do you know how most writers respond to that question?"

She shook her head.

"Some will say that they become inspired by observing humanity; by watching people go about their daily lives. Others will *say* they get their ideas from dreams or from watching a sunset, while taking a shower or walking their *dog*, for Christ sake." He glared at her for a moment, seemingly upset by what he had just shared with her and then spoke softly, again.

"Would you believe any of those explanations, Miss Wentworth?"

She shrugged her shoulders and replied, "Why

shouldn't I?"

"Because they're all a load of *crap*, that's why," he hissed.

Taken aback by his somewhat odd behavior, she asked, "Just why was it you requested this interview today?"

"Because I'm going to die, soon," he told her, bluntly. "But, before I do, I need to get something off my chest and what I have to tell will set the literary world back on its heels and quite possibly ruin a great number of people, many of whom I once counted as friends."

Finally sensing a story here, possibly a very big story, Miss Wentworth leaned forward. "Please, go on."

"Did you know that I am fifty-two years old?" he asked, and could easily tell by the look on her face she had been unaware of that fact. "Yes, yes, I know I look much closer to eighty years old than I do to fifty, but if you had done your homework and checked my bio before coming here, you would know that I'm telling the truth."

Now actually shocked by his appearance, she stammered, "But, what...I mean, how—"

"How did I come to be such a physical wreck," he waved an emaciated arm at himself, "in such a short period of time?"

"Well, yes. I think that might be a legitimate question which my readers would want an answer to," she said, thinking immediately of drug and/or alcohol abuse as a possible reason for his pathetic appearance, or perhaps it was some rare, wasting disease that he might have picked up in a foreign country while doing research for one of his stories. She wondered vaguely if whatever he had gotten might be contagious and leaned farther back into the sofa.

She noted her movement and snorted. "You needn't worry that what I have is catching, my dear," he told her. "You would have to be a much better writer than you are to suffer from what I am afflicted with. No offense meant, of course," he added.

She smiled weakly at the insult. "Of course," she said, softly.

He grunted, grabbed the wheels of his chair and propelled himself over to a sideboard, "Would you care for a drink?"

"No, thank you, not while I'm working," she replied, but then thought better of the suggestion. "As a matter of fact, I would like a drink. Whiskey, please. Neat."

"Ahh, a woman after me own heart," he cackled and poured out two glasses of dark, amber liquid from a crystal decanter. He set the drinks on a tray in his lap and wheeled himself back over to the table. He held a glass out to her, then placed the tray down and held up his own glass, "To getting even," he said.

She raised an eyebrow at the toast, but nodded and they both drank.

"Should you really be drinking in your, um, condition?" she asked.

He cackled again, drinking heavily himself. "Alcohol had nothing to do with my *condition*— apparently enjoying it, too," he said. "My doctor says I can drink as much as I want to. It helps me cope. Since there's no hope anyway," he added.

She leaned forward, elbows on knees, her hands wrapped around her glass. "Why are you dying?" she asked.

He took another sip from his glass and stared intently at her, "Because I've had most of my life force drained out of me over the last twenty-five years and there isn't enough left to keep me going for much longer."

She frowned and shook her head, slightly. "I don't understand."

"Few people do at this point, but I aim to remedy that lack of understanding before I go," he said and tilting his head back, finished off his drink. He wiped his mouth with the back of his hand and set the empty glass down on the table. "What I am going to tell you will be hard to believe, I know—hell, I didn't believe it at first, either—but the evidence will prove me right, you wait and see.

"To begin with, I always wanted to be a writer— mainly short stories and then, of course, novels. I started writing seriously when I was about twenty-five years old. I was just out of college and thought I would be engaged with my writing career for some time— don't forget, this was thirty years ago. Oh, I sold a short story here and there, maybe two or three a year and made a couple of bucks, but I couldn't find the *edge*, you know? Something was missing from my style of writing that would land me that one, big break—or so I thought. Turns out I was right about missing something, but not nearly in the way I first imagined."

Miss Wentworth nodded encouragement and took another sip of her whiskey.

"I started attending writing seminars in Southern California and met a number of well-known authors. For some reason, a few of them took a liking to me and offered to help me polish some of my work. I jumped at the chance, of course—these guys were like heroes to me. Hell, I had been reading some of their work since I was a kid." He leaned forward in his chair and began rubbing his hands together, nervously.

"One night, I was invited to a party up in the hills above Santa Monica. Someone had just signed a big book deal and was celebrating, so I just tagged along. I was only about twenty-four and was still in awe of most of these guys. The party lasted most of the night and by the time it broke up, everyone was pretty plastered. I was rather tipsy myself, you know, but I wasn't drunk—didn't want to risk making a fool of myself in front of all my heroes." He paused and sighed, then added, softly, "I didn't start drinking heavily until a few years later."

He looked up and caught her eyes with his own. "Have you ever noticed how most really good writers are always flawed in some way? Serious problems with drugs or alcohol, for instance? Deviant sexual requirements or eccentric behavior that is explained away simply because they're gifted artists?" She nodded and gave him a wan smile. "They were keeping a secret that made many of them go mad, commit suicide or at the very least seek shelter from

102

that knowledge in a bottle, in drugs or in some other perversion. I mean, even as far back as Poe and Lewis Carroll or Sir Arthur Conan Doyle, H.P. Lovecraft and Robert E. Howard—all of them were literary time bombs and the writers of today are no exception. Why do you suppose that is, Miss Wentworth?"

She shrugged her shoulders. "I… I have no idea," she said.

"Ahh, but that's the answer, right there," he told her excitedly, pointing a shriveled finger in her direction. "*The very idea* is the key!"

She shook her head, slowly. "I'm sorry, but you lost me."

"Of course I did," he said and calmed down a little, settling himself more comfortably in his chair. "As I was saying, everyone was quite drunk at this party and I overheard a couple of people talking—in what they thought were hushed tones, I'm sure—about this 'place' where they obtained the ideas for their stories. One of them was saying the cost was becoming more than he could bear, but he hadn't had a bestselling book for several years and might just have to go back for a decent idea, no matter what the price. Now, I didn't understand any of this, but was just drunk enough not to know any better, so I asked them what they were talking about.

"When they saw who I was, they both became unglued over the fact that I had been eavesdropping, although they had been talking so loudly, I'm sure most of the room overheard their conversation—at the time, I didn't realize all of the other writers who were there already knew what they had been talking about. Anyway, this one guy jumps up and then he was all over me, knocking me down and threatening to kill me if I ever spoke a word to anyone about what I had overheard. It took three men to pull him off of me and calm him down."

He paused and began wringing his hands together, again. "I was taken aside by a friend and warned to never, *ever*, bring up what I had heard. I agreed, of course, even though I wasn't sure what they had actually been talking about. I basically forgot all about the incident, until some three weeks later, when the guy who had gone off on me committed suicide. He was a fairly well known author and it was a big scandal at the time, although in today's news market that kind of death wouldn't garner nearly as much play in the press as it did then.

"That writer's death reminded me of what I had heard him talking about at the party and I became curious." He shrugged his shoulders. "Would that I had left well enough alone, but I was young and thought I was invincible. I went to some of the authors I knew, telling them that I really wanted to write a great novel—just *one*, I told them and I would be happy. Every single one of them smiled when I said that and nearly all of them told me the same thing. 'You can't be happy with just *one* good novel, kid. Once you've got the bug, it's like an addiction and you can't let it go. You have to keep writing or you just curl up and die.'

"So, I asked each of them if the writer who had

recently killed himself had 'curled up'. Only one of them had the guts to answer that question for me. Harlan was—oh, crap, I wasn't supposed to use any real names. You won't print that, will you?"

"Not if you don't want me to," Miss Wentworth told him.

"All right. Good. He's still alive you know and wouldn't appreciate my bringing his name into this."

"It's no problem, honestly," she assured him.

"All right," he repeated. Miss Wentworth noted that he appeared to be becoming more and more nervous as he continued his story. "Well, this... author friend of mine was a bit of a queer duck, even back then. He was already a famous writer who had even worked on television scripts back in the 60s and was only a few years older than myself. He knew what it was like to want to break into the big-time and decided to take me under his wing and show me the ropes—the *real* ropes, as he and other successful writers knew them.

"He warned me that what he was going to share with me had to be held in the strictest confidence. Only a select group of people knew about this and I had to swear an oath to keep silent about what I would soon learn, on forfeit of my very life if I ever disclosed this secret to an outsider."

"So, you are breaking that oath, now, by talking about this to me?" she asked, quietly.

"Yes. Yes, I am," he said and looked quickly over his shoulder toward the front door, then back again. "But, I'm doing so to perhaps help some young, aspiring writer avoid the pitfalls and horrors that I and many

105

other authors have become so deeply entangled with."

"And, you are willing to perhaps forfeit your life by telling this—and how would that come about, by the way?" she asked, somewhat skeptical of his whole story.

"I have already told you, my dear," he said, nodding his head. "My life force is slowly being drained away and eventually, there won't be enough left to keep me alive." He coughed as he finished speaking—a loose, rattling cough that lasted several seconds. Putting a hand to his mouth and wiping away some spittle, he said, "Excuse me."

He sighed, again and then continued. "You have no *idea*—ah, there's that word again—how what I have to tell will affect some people's reputations, and their lives and livelihoods as well, should this become public. But, it must become public. Oh, I'm sure that if I were not so close to death right now, my body would be found soon after this story is published, no doubt made to appear a messy suicide. But, since I will soon be dead of my demise, there should be no repercussions to myself. And, as I have no offspring, I have no fear of harm coming to anyone close to me, once I'm gone."

"What about me?" she asked, suddenly becoming concerned for her own welfare, just on the off chance he was telling the truth. "Will I be in any danger if this information is published?" She wasn't even sure, as yet, exactly what he was getting at with this story, but she could tell that he was quite serious about fearing retribution against himself for speaking to her and if there was even a remote possibility of that danger being turned toward her, she wanted to know about it.

After a moment, he said, "I shouldn't think so. Your story will be considered second hand information, after all, but you might consider using a pseudonym for this piece, at least until after the excitement and blood-letting dies down."

"Just until after the 'blood-letting' dies down. Wonderful," she said, with just a touch of sarcasm. "I don't even know if this story is worth the risk or not, assuming there really is a risk."

He leaned forward and with a twinkle in his eye, asked softly, "Would you risk it for a possible *Pulitzer?*"

She gasped, a hand going to her throat. "You're kidding, right?"

He shook his head and leaned back in his chair. "I am, in fact, quite serious. This story will blow the lid off the literary world and whoever breaks it will become instantly famous and awards are a shoe-in." Then he smiled and added, "I kid you not."

Oddly enough, she believed him. She wasn't sure just why, but she did believe him. He was a respected writer after all, with a dozen bestsellers under his belt, and looking at him now she couldn't see any reason for him to be stringing her along. True, he had been somewhat of a recluse for a number of years, but considering his condition, she could understand why he had chosen that lifestyle and wanted to avoid the public eye. And, for some reason, she trusted him. "Okay," she decided. "Fire away."

TERRY D. SCHEERER

He sighed and turned his gaze toward the softly crackling fire, tucked beneath a low mantle. For a moment she thought that he had changed his mind about talking to her, but after a few seconds, he continued. "I was told that there was a place—an actual *place*, mind you—where authors could go to obtain ideas for great short stories and bestselling novels. I didn't believe him, of course, but he assured me that what he was telling me was not only true, but that this place had been used by famous authors for hundreds of years, if not longer."

Turning back toward her, Miss Wentworth thought that he was looking somewhat more haggard than when she had arrived, but it could have just been a trick of the light and shadows playing over his face.

"Knowledge of its existence," he said, his voice actually sounding stronger than before, "had been passed by word of mouth for generations, each one sharing the secret with another, down through the ages. Several years ago, hardly anyone knew about this 'place' and, as you can find out for yourself if you research older literature, there wasn't an overwhelming amount of really good novels written back then."

He paused, this time a little longer than the previous episode and she waited to see if he'd spit something out of him. He wiped at his mouth once again and this time she noticed small flakes of skin were rubbed from his lips and fell down into his lap.

He coughed, again, this time a little longer than the previous episode and it appeared to really take something out of him. He wiped at his mouth with the back of his hand and she noticed small flakes of skin were rubbed off his face and floated gently down into his lap.

"Oh, there were always a few writers of quality, in every generation," he continued, his voice somewhat raspy, now. "But, back then it was a more closely guarded secret than today. People like Shakespeare knew about it, of course, as did such writers as Melville and Stoker, Washington Irving, Twain, Dickens, Poe and a few others. Take Jules Verne and H.G. Wells, for example. Those two were a hundred years ahead of their time with the stories of space and time travel they penned, not to mention all of the marvelous inventions they came up with for their stories." He looked hard at her, but his eyes didn't seem quite able to focus. "Do you believe they just *happened* to think those stories up all on their own, when no one else in the entire world was writing about such things?" He grunted and nodded his head, slightly. "I'll leave that decision up to you, after I finish what I have to say."

He wiped at his mouth, where a thin line of spittle was forming. But, leaving them aside, it wasn't until the middle of the twentieth century that more and more writers were learning of the secret. The huge explosion of great authors in the forties, fifties and sixties begs the fact that those people *had* to have stumbled onto something that gave them all an edge. Remember the 'edge' I mentioned earlier—the one that I felt I needed to catch a break in the field? Well, this *place* was definitely it and no mistake about it."

Miss Wentworth nodded and smiled slightly, even though she was becoming concerned by the way he looked. It appeared as if he had aged another few years just since she met him, less than thirty minutes ago. The skin about his face seemed to hang loosely from his skull and there appeared to be little, if any muscle tone beneath the sagging flesh. His eyes, that had seemed so bright when he first started talking, now looked cloudy and dull. He wiped a shaky hand over his face, causing a small flurry of skin flakes to shower down around him and his head was now bobbing slightly, as he tried to continue.

"I was taken there, late one night by Har—by my friend. He told me he needed another good idea for a short story he had to write, for some magazine or other. Seems you could also pick up ideas for short stories from this place, at a much-reduced price.

"We left his apartment, just off Hollywood Boulevard, a little before midnight and walked down to the end of the block. There were a bunch of stores along this part of the street, all of them closed up for the night—all except one. This one store front had all of the windows and the glass door blacked over, as if it were out of business, but there was a light coming from under the door. I was told not to question anything I saw inside the store, not to interfere with anything that I might witness and not to attempt to leave the store without him. I nervously agreed and he opened the door and we walked inside."

The old man rubbed the back of his neck for a moment, then began wringing his hands, once again.

"We entered a room that was quite long, narrow and poorly lit. The first thing that struck me odd was the walls. They were covered, from floor to ceiling, with a lattice-work of small pigeon holes and each little hole contained a glass vial, about the same size and shape of an old fashioned light bulb—bulbous at the top and tapering down to a wide opening, which appeared to be stopped with a large cork. There must have been thousands of these things, all tucked neatly away, in their little niches. There were also a number of library-style ladders, the kind that have rollers on the top, leaning against the walls and they stretched up toward the ceiling, which was lost in the gloom."

As he paused to lick his thin, nearly colorless lips, Miss Wentworth asked softly, "May I get you another drink?"

"Mmm, yes, yes," he said. "I, I would appreciate that...very much, I think." She took his glass to the sideboard and poured out a half glass of whiskey. When she brought it back to him, his hand was shaking so badly, she had to steady the glass for him so he could take a sip.

"Would you like to rest a bit, before going on?" she asked, becoming genuinely concerned for his well being. He seemed to have lost more strength, just in the last few minutes.

"No!" he replied, emphatically. "I must get this all out, while I still can." He began coughing again and noticing a box of tissues on a small table next to the sofa, she pulled loose a few and handed them to him, then set his glass down on the table in front of his

111

chair. He managed a weak, "Thank you," after the coughing fit was over.

Miss Wentworth turned the tape cassette over in her recorder and said, "You may continue whenever you're ready."

"Yes, well," he said, wiping at his mouth with the wad of tissue. "I remember being terrified, even though I didn't know why I should have been. We went a bit farther into the dimly lit room and I noticed several tables—looked like stripped down operating tables—lined up in the center of the room. Toward the back, one of the tables seemed to be occupied. I was about to say something when someone appeared next to me and gave me quite a start."

"I jumped, but it was just a little old man. He only came up to about my shoulder and certainly looked harmless enough, but he gave off such an aura of evil that I was afraid to be close to him. Bald and wearing thick glasses, the old man just looked at me for a moment, then turned to my friend. It seemed that they knew each other, as they began an immediate, hushed conversation and the old man soon led us to one of the closer tables. My friend pulled off his shirt and climbed onto the table, lying down on his back.

"At the head of the table was a metal cap arrangement, with wires coming from it. The cap thing was fit over my friend's head and he just lay there, while the old man vanished for a few moments. My friend smiled up at me and then gave me a wink, as if to imply everything was fine.

"Waiting for the old man to return, I looked around

and saw that there was someone else on a table farther back in the room. They seemed to be just lying there, with the metal cap thing attached to their head. I wanted a better look, but the old man reappeared next to the table, holding one of those bulbous glass vials in his hand. He touched a spot on my friend's abdomen, just below and to the right of his navel, then placed the vial, open end down, against his skin."

Miss Wentworth, in spite of herself, was becoming intrigued with this story. She finished off her own whiskey, waiting for the old writer to catch his breath and continue. She noticed that he was beginning to wheeze slightly, now, with each breath.

"My friend closed his eyes and I could tell that he was gritting his teeth. His fists were clenched tightly and sweat began to bead his forehead—he appeared to be in some sort of pain. All the while, the old man was smiling and lightly tapping the glass vial, as he hummed some weird tune beneath his breath. My friend moaned a couple of times and I just stood there, transfixed, not knowing what was happening or what I should do about it. Then he gasped, just once and the old man removed the vial and quickly stuffed a cork into the opening.

"After that, my friend just sagged limply against the table, but seemed to be all right, if somewhat exhausted. The old man, meanwhile, was holding the vial up to the light, smiling and lightly shaking the glass. I couldn't see anything inside the bulb, but thought I heard a faint scratching sound, like tiny claws on glass. The old man moved over to a wall and placed the vial in an empty niche, then came back and adjusted some dials on the metal cap and flicked a switch on the side of it. My friend gave me a weak smile and then closed his eyes for a few minutes."

He paused and took a few deep, shaky breaths, before going on. "As I stood there, looking down at him, I noticed a red, circular welt forming where the vial had been placed over his skin. I also saw several other, similar scars, each about the size of a half dollar, scattered over his abdomen and chest area."

The frail author paused and lightly shook his head, as if trying to shake loose some memory. Miss Wentworth leaned forward and helped him take another sip of whiskey. He appeared to be getting weaker by the moment, but she didn't bother trying to stop him from speaking.

"We finally got out of there, but the experience unnerved me, I must say. I was an emotional wreck, while my good pal seemed fine and was very excited about this new idea he had for a story. I didn't see him for several months after that—I was almost afraid to— but then his story was published and it was terrific, just as all of his other work always seemed to be. I looked him up after reading his story and we talked for the first time about our trip to the 'idea store'. That was when I decided that I wanted to write a serious novel and we went back to the 'store' for the first of many great ideas I acquired from that place."

He started coughing again, a longer and more hacking series of coughs that left him noticeably weaker. "I had no *idea* how painful the process was going to be, but my friend assured me that the pain would only last a short while, but fame would last a lifetime. He was right about that. My first novel was published just about a year later and you know how well it was received. Since that first visit, more than twenty-five years ago, I have gone back to that mysterious place at least a couple of dozen times for story and novel ideas. And for each idea that I received, a bit more of my life force was drained from me and stored in one of those little glass vials."

He smiled, weakly. "At the time, I didn't think losing those little bits of life would bother me all that much; I was still young and strong, after all. Granted, you're always weak after a session, but the new ideas running around in your head give you such a...well, it's like a week-long adrenaline rush. You don't want to eat or sleep—you just want to write. If you haven't experienced that thrill of taking a new idea and writing it out, forming it into a completed story, well, I can't explain it to you. It's something you have to experience, first hand.

"Understand that not just anyone can go in and obtain an idea, then write a bestseller with it. You must have *some* innate talent. You have to be able to put sentences together to form coherent thoughts and build characters that people want to read about, but once you have the initial idea, well, that's half the battle, right there."

He paused again, and Miss Wentworth took the opportunity to speak. "And, what happened to all of those vials of your 'life force', or for that matter, any of the other vials that were stored within this place?"

He chuckled, weakly. "I didn't know what was to be done with the life force that was taken from me back then and I didn't really care. All I cared about were the ideas that I received and what I could do with them." He sighed, then; a deep, drawn-out sigh that seemed to deflate him. "For years I kept going back to obtain new ideas, not worrying about the damage I might be causing myself. Those boys were right, so long ago, when they said writing was like an addiction. I was hooked, just as surely as if I had been taking hard drugs.

"Ten years ago, I grew weary of the rat race and I tried to stop writing for a while. Within a month I became so sick, I had to be hospitalized. Turned out I had lost bone density, muscle tone and short-term memory function, all seemingly overnight. The doctors didn't know what was wrong with me, but I knew. I knew that if I wanted to stay alive, I would have to return for another 'idea' and start writing again. So, I went back and wrote another bestseller. Then, to appease my addiction, I kept going back, writing another novel just about every year since then and my health was fine until just six months ago, when I decided that enough was enough."

He smiled, but Miss Wentworth could tell that the effort was painful for him. "I haven't written so much as a birthday greeting since then and you can see, I've aged more than twenty years in the past few months. My body is rebelling against me, it seems. The life force that was taken from me during all of those visits is now coming back to haunt me. I no longer have enough energy to keep myself alive for very much longer."

Miss Wentworth slowly shook her head. "As fascinating as all of this is, it just doesn't seem…well, quite real. I'm sure you can understand my position."

Waving a weak hand, he said, "Yes, of course. I told you I didn't even believe it at first."

"Well, take the location of this 'idea place', for example," she said. "If you found it somewhere in the Hollywood area, couldn't anyone just wander in off the street and see what's going on in there?"

He cackled, weakly, then coughed and wiped his mouth with the sleeve of his shirt. "It isn't in Hollywood, Miss Wentworth, any more than it is in New York City or in Wichita, Kansas. It is in all of those places and in none of them."

"Um…I'm afraid you lost me, again."

"Don't you get it? What I'm talking about is something magical, something perhaps supernatural; something that is obviously not of this earth, something we just have no clue about. That *place*, whatever it may be, will always be wherever someone wants it to be. I could walk out my front door right now—that is, if I could still walk—and it would be a couple of blocks down the street from here. An author in England or France, in Russia or in Podunk, Iowa, could walk two blocks from their home and there it would be, waiting for them. I have visited this 'store' while doing research in other countries, so I know of what I speak. It is just *there*, whenever or wherever an author needs it to be."

117

His ranting seemed to have winded him and while he was catching his breath, she said, "That seems a bit hard to believe, don't you think?"

Wheezing heavily, he managed to growl, "The whole bloody thing is hard to believe and I've lived through it. So far, at least," he added, weakly. "I have seen plenty of other writers in that place, too. Well-known authors, all of them—from queens of romance novels to the 'King' of modern day horror. Where do you think he got that idea to go visit a hotel in the Colorado Mountains?"

"Still and all, this is just so much hearsay."

He really seemed to be having trouble catching his breath now—he was almost gulping air, like a fish out of water. "Here, let me…show you…something," he gasped. Removing the cloth cap he had been wearing, he exposed a balding pate with thin wisps of hair attached to it in several spots. He lowered his head and with a shaky finger, pointed to the top of his head. "Look."

She stood and tried to peer closely at the mottled skin that was nearly translucent against his skull. Then she saw what he wanted her to see. There, in a loose triangle, were three small circular scars, each about the size of a half dollar. "Oh," was all she could say.

"I have more than twenty other scars… just like those… on other parts of my body," he told her, his voice now quaking with the effort to speak. "Would you…like…to see them?"

"Uh, no, I don't think I need to see any more," she said, reseating herself on the sofa.

The cap dropped from his limp fingers and his arm slipped off the wheelchair armrest. "It's happening… quicker…than I thought…it would," he wheezed. He began coughing again, a deep rattling cough that sounded as if things were being shaken loose inside his chest. She had never heard a 'death rattle' before, but she was sure that it must sound very much like what she was now hearing.

Seeing that the old man was really in trouble, she got up and moved around the table, to stand next to him. "Is there anything I can do," she asked, helplessly.

He stopped coughing, finally, but looked pale and drawn. Drool was running down his chin and his eyes were unfocused, his head bobbing up and down with each wracking breath.

"It's…too late," he managed to whisper. "They… must know…what I'm doing. Talking…to you. They know…I've told…you…everything."

"What are you talking about?" she asked, rather too loudly, as fear was beginning to creep into her voice. "Who are *they?*"

"Them!" he wheezed. "The ones…from the…from that *place*. They're using my…my stored life force…to drain off…what I have…left," he whispered, his voice rapidly failing.

There was a sudden series of loud, sharp *bangs* against the front door and Miss Wentworth jumped nearly a foot off the floor. "What's that?" she hissed, startled and now thoroughly frightened.

The author's head lolled onto one shoulder and a thin trickle of blood was now leaking from his lips.

119

"Get…out," he gasped, as someone rattled the doorknob on the front door.

"Oh, my god!" she cried. "What's happening?"

"They've…come…for…me," he whispered, his voice barely audible.

There was a frantic pounding on the front door and the doorknob rattled, furiously.

"My god, *my god, my GOD!*" she cried, looking quickly from the door, down to her host and back to the door, again.

"Quick," the author wheezed. "Out…the…back." His head fell forward onto his chest and then the wheezing stopped.

"Oh, *shit!*" she whispered, her hands against the sides of her face. This was just too damn much, she decided, but was at a loss as to what she should do. The sharp sound of splintering wood coming from the area of the front door helped her make a decision. She grabbed up her purse and headed for the back of the house. Just as she was going through the doorway to the hall, she remembered her tape recorder.

It sounded as if the front door was being torn apart and she absolutely did not want to meet whatever was causing that type of destruction. Whimpering in fright, she dashed back into the room and snatched up the recorder, pausing just long enough to give a quick look at the dead author, then she was through the door and down the hall.

Regardless of how absurd the story might have sounded to her originally, she now realized that she did, in fact, believe everything the old man had told her. Clutching the small recorder to her chest, she knew that in her hand she had the story of a lifetime—she just needed to stay alive long enough to write it.

Panting from fear and exertion, she ran through the kitchen and out the back door, into a huge, darkened yard. Looking around frantically, she ran across the yard, ducked under the low branches of a spreading pine tree and huddled in the protective shadows behind its trunk.

She waited for several minutes, barely breathing, but heard no further noise from the house. Feeling it was safe to move again, she carefully tucked the tape recorder inside her purse. 'I made it', she thought and clutched the purse tightly to her chest. 'By god, this story will make me *famous!*' Then she frowned. Who would ever actually believe such a crackpot story was true? It would never work, she decided; not without corroborating evidence, which she obviously did not have. What might work, however, would be a fictionalized version of the story. Hell, the whole thing sounded like science fiction, anyway, mixed with equal parts of horror and the supernatural. It *would* work!

Miss Wentworth smiled to herself. Yes, that's the way to go with this. I could turn this mess into a short story or maybe a novella. Hell, with a little work, it might even stretch itself into a *novel*, for crying out loud! Somewhat pleased with herself for managing to possibly salvage something from, well, almost nothing, she realized there was one other thing that she would require to make this plan become a reality.

"What I need," she said, softly, to herself, "is a way

121

to bring this all together. What I need to make this work is just one, really good idea."

Miss Wentworth sensed a sudden, unmistakably evil presence close to her in the shadows and looked quickly to her right. She nearly fainted when she saw a short, bald man with thick glasses looking up at her. He was smiling slightly and in one hand held a small glass vial, shaped remarkably like an old fashioned light bulb.

"You called?" he asked, quietly.

Then she fainted.

-

Band of Gold

The following story is not a 'Horror' story in the classical sense. I suppose it could fall under the category of a 'Ghost' story, even though the spirit in question does not put in an actual appearance. Nevertheless, this is one of my favorite stories, because so much of the background is based upon fact. The ring described in this story does exist, exactly as it is described. I own the ring and it came into my possession a few years ago, much the same way it is noted in this story. I wrote this piece for the same reasons the main character describes why he bought the ring, which is, in fact, why I purchased it. How much of the remainder of the story is fact and how much is fiction is somewhat open to debate.

In the meantime, I am still waiting to hear from the owner of this...

Band of Gold

CHRIS WAS JUST finishing his lunch as a friend slid into the booth across from him. "Hey, Matt," he said, wiping his mouth with a crumpled paper napkin.

"Chris," Matt replied with a nod, an odd sort of smile on his face.

"What's up?"

Matt looked rather cautiously around the diner, as if to be sure they weren't being observed. Satisfied, he removed a ring from the finger of his right hand and held it out to Chris. "Check this out," he told him, quietly, but there was an undertone of excitement in his voice.

Chris wiped his hands on another napkin and took the ring. He knew that Matt collected small articles of silver and gold as a sort of part-time hobby. His father had gotten him started on it a few years ago and now, whenever Matt had some extra money, he would prowl the local pawnshops and thrift stores looking for silver coins and old gold jewelry. Chris had seen several of the more interesting items that Matt had picked up over the years, but this one just looked like a plain, gold wedding band. After he had turned it over a few times he said, "Very nice. Fourteen carat?"

"Eighteen," Matt said, that peculiar smile still plastered across his face. "Read the inscription."

Chris angled the ring toward the window to pick up the light and squinted at the inside of the thin band. His eyebrows arched as he saw the writing.

"Wow. It's written in script," he commented, surprised.

"Yeah. They don't do that kind of work any more. Read it out loud."

Chris turned the ring to find the beginning of the inscription. He saw the 18K stamp and then the words began. "'I love you more than you love me.'" he read. Then there was a date stamped into the ring: '6/22/46'.

"Wow, that's wicked," he said, softly. Looking up at Matt, he handed the ring back and asked, "Where'd you find this?"

Matt took the band and pushed it back onto his right ring finger. "Over at the Mine Shaft Jewelry Exchange, about a week ago." He began to slowly turn the ring around and around his finger, but didn't seem aware of the action.

"Must have an interesting story behind it," Chris said, watching the ring rotate around his friend's finger.

"You don't know the half of it," Matt told him in a quiet voice.

"Why? What do you mean?"

Matt didn't say anything for a moment, then looked quickly behind him to see if anyone was seated in the next booth. It was empty. He leaned toward Chris and spoke softly. "Ever since I put this ring on, I've been... well, seeing things," he said.

Chris leaned forward, too, more to humor his friend than to keep what they were saying private. "Seeing things, like what? Visions? Ghosts? Britney Spears, naked?"

"No, nothing like that," Matt said, leaning back and shaking his head. "Maybe *seeing* things isn't the right way to put it. It's more like I'm *remembering* these things, but they're someone else's memories."

Chris frowned, realizing that Matt was serious about this. "How can you tell?"

"Because, I'm remembering things that obviously happened years ago—most of them before I was even born and these are memories I should have no knowledge of."

Curious now and also a bit concerned for his friend's state of mind, Chris asked, "Where do you think these unusual recollections are coming from?"

"That's just it," Matt said in a hushed voice, looking down to where he was slowly rotating the gold band around his finger. "I think they're coming from the ring, itself."

Chris leaned back and placed his hands on the table. "Now, wait a minute, dude. What makes you think *anything*, let alone a bunch of vivid memories are coming from that ring?"

Matt looked up, sharply. "They aren't *wild* memories," he snapped.

"Okay, okay, sorry," Chris said, holding up his hands in mock surrender. "I didn't mean anything by it."

"I *know*," Matt told him and sighed. "It's just been a really crazy week."

"No problem." Chris couldn't remember ever seeing his friend wound up this tightly, before. "So, why not just start from the beginning. When exactly did these memories first hit you?"

Matt leaned back and dropped his hands into his lap. Even though Chris could no longer see what he was doing, he felt sure that his friend was still unconsciously turning the ring around and around his finger as he began the story.

"Like I said, I got the ring about a week ago. I bought it specifically because of the inscription, because, well, you know, it just seemed so *sad*."

He sighed again and leaned forward. "Here was some poor dude's wedding ring, from a man and learned that, well, there was some poor dude's wedding ring. It must have been the band of some major love story—one that had known both happiness and sorrow, love and many family memories—tragedies and triumphs. And nobody even gave a shit about the pain—and joy—that was bound up in it, just through wearing it. And the person who once owned the ring was now gone, though *someone* should have

128

loved them..."

Chris smiled, slightly, knowing that beneath the scruffy beard and the many tattoos that covered most of his arms, Matt was really a sentimental kind of guy, but he didn't let many people see that side of himself. "Yeah, go on."

"Anyway, I took it home and didn't even try it on until later that night." He began rotating the ring around his finger, yet again, as he continued. "The ring fit my right ring finger perfectly and almost as soon as I put it on, I began to have these weird flashes of something almost like memory. Just bits and pieces at first—I thought I was remembering something from my own past. But after a while, I realized that I *didn't* have any memories of that kind of wedding."

"You remembered a wedding?"

"Yeah. It was his wedding," Matt said, holding up the ring for Chris to see, as if he had forgotten what it looked like in the past few minutes. "The actual guy who owned this ring."

"How do you know it was, well, his ring," Chris asked, nodding toward Matt's hand.

"I saw the ring—*this* ring," he said, making a fist and bringing the band close to Chris's face, "being placed on his finger. I saw his bride and the ring he gave her. I felt them kiss, dude, and I actually *felt*, somewhere deep down inside of me, the incredible love that he had for her."

Chris leaned away from the fist that hovered inches from his nose and slowly nodded. "So, the first memories were of his wedding, then?"

129

Matt brought his fist down to the table and covered it with his other hand, as if to protect the ring from further exposure. "Yeah," he answered, in a more calm voice. "It must have been the first time he ever put the ring on, so that's where all of the memories start from."

"What else do you remember about this guy?"

"A lot. Nearly his whole life came to me, eventually —the important bits and pieces of it, anyhow. I… well, I was kind of freaked out at first, you know. Didn't understand what was happening, so I took the ring off that night after the wedding memories hit me and didn't put it back on again until the next day."

Chris nodded. "And then what happened?"

"It was like the ring sensed that I was freaked by what had happened the night before, or something. Anyway, the memories came more slowly and seemed more coherent, this time. I was able to follow what I was seeing and it all began to make sense to me. Sort of."

"Okay. And how long did this memory session last?"

"Sessions, actually," Matt said. "I was only able to stand an hour or so, a few times a day, at first, but it stretched into four or five hour sessions, a couple of times a day, after a while. It took about five days, altogether."

Chris shook his head, still finding all of this hard to believe. He had known Matt for years, however, and had never known him to be the kind of person who would shovel loads of crap around to his friends, especially something as outlandish as this story

130

appeared to be. Wanting to give him the benefit of the doubt, he said, "All right, do you think you can give me an abridged version of what you found out about this guy?"

"Yeah, I think so." Matt sighed again, then continued. "It didn't all come in any kind of order. I mean, the memories were all kind of jumbled up and it took me a while to figure out the proper sequence, you know, but it goes something like this:

"Ted—Theodore, actually, but he liked Ted, better— and his future wife, they grew up on the same street in a small town in Oregon. They were a couple of months apart in age, so they went to the same schools, they played together as they were growing up, their parents hung out together—the two of them were really close. By the time they reached high school, they were, you know, going steady."

"Going steady?" Chris asked with a smile.

"Dude, don't forget, this was back in the 1940s," Matt reminded him.

"Oh, yeah," he said, the smile vanishing. "Go on."

"They had been in love for years and had planned to get married right after high school, but then the war broke out." He saw the blank expression on his friend's face, so he added, "The Second World War? You remember, we studied a chapter on it in our high school history class?"

Chris smiled. "Oh, yeah, dude, I remember. John Wayne and Iwo Jima. The Atom Bomb. That war, right?"

"Right. Well, Ted wanted to join up right away, but

his father insisted that he finish high school, so he joined the Army the day after his graduation in 1943. Shirley—that was his girlfriend's name—was worried about him, but understood and supported his decision to join up and said she'd wait for him, no matter how long he was gone. The day he left, he told her he loved her and said, "I love you more than you love me."

"Hey, that's the inscription in the ring."

"Yeah. That's how he signed all of her letters to him, too, the whole time he was away. It was like her special way of saying, 'I love you.' She once said that seeing the ring so he would be reminded every day just how much she really loved him." Matt was slowly turning the ring around his finger as he spoke, a far away look on his face, as if he had actually been a part of the experience he was telling Chris.

"So," he finally continued, "Ted went off to boot camp and then was shipped out to Italy in time for Thanksgiving in '43. He missed the Allied invasion of Salerno by a couple of months, but there was still a lot of fighting going on when he arrived. Lucky for him, he spent most of the winter guarding German prisoners of war near Naples, but eventually his company was moved north and after several bloody months, they fought their way through France and into Germany. That was when they got the worst of it. The Germans really had their backs up against a wall and they threw everything they had at Ted and his buddies. He saw an awful lot of his friends and comrades die during those months. What was left of his company had managed to battle their way clear to the outskirts

132

of Berlin when the Germans finally surrendered."

"Wow," Chris said. "I can't even imagine living through that kind of stuff."

"I don't have to imagine it," Matt told him, quietly. "I remember all of it, as if I had been there. That is, I remember it through Ted, or at least through his ring," he said, looking down at the seemingly simple gold band. Chris looked up and asked, "Dude, are you all right?"

"Yeah, it's just hard reliving all these memories, again." A waitress was passing by and Matt held up his hand. "Say, could I get a cola or something?"

"Sure," she replied and looked at Chris. "You want anything else?"

"No, I'm good, thanks."

"Okay. Be right back."

"Thanks," Matt said as she left.

"So, you want to take a break or something, with the story?"

"Naw, I'm all right," Matt told him, but sighed again before continuing. "Anyway, by the time Ted got shipped back to the States, it was early in 1946 and the war was finally over, so after filling out paperwork for a few weeks, he was discharged from the service in March of that year."

The waitress arrived with his drink and he took a long swallow before going on. "Things were going pretty well for him, then. Shirley was waiting for him, just like he knew she would be and they started planning the wedding as soon as he caught his breath. They were married on June 22, 1946."

"Like it says in the ring," Chris noted.

"Right. So, it turned out one of Ted's uncles was in the insurance business and he got his foot in the door early, there. What with all of the guys coming home from the war and starting their own families, insurance became a booming business and Ted got in on the ground floor, so to speak. The company was based in Los Angeles, so they moved down to Southern California after the wedding. He used his GI Bill to buy a house and they settled in to make a life for themselves and start a family."

Matt stopped to take another drink and Chris said, "And all of this information came to you from the ring?"

"I don't know where else it could have come from," he admitted. "I never heard of these people until I put this ring on and there was too much detail in the memories for this to be just my imagination."

"Well, I don't mean to sound insensitive or anything, but are you sure these people really existed?"

Matt smiled. "Yeah, I'm sure. I checked with the cemetery where they're both buried and sure enough, there they were; Ted and Shirley Sterling, resting quietly in adjoining plots."

"Jeez, dude, you know where they're buried?"

"Yeah, I do. It turns out that's a rather important aspect of this whole story."

"How come?" Chris asked, almost afraid to know the answer.

"I'll tell you, but that would be getting ahead of myself." He leaned back and took up the story from where he had left off. "Ted and Shirley were a perfect couple and they loved each other, unconditionally and completely. The economy boomed after the war and things were good here at home. Ted did really well in the insurance business and moved up in the company. They had four kids—three boys and a girl, but one of their sons died of scarlet fever in 1952."

"Oh, bummer."

"Yeah, I know, but aside from that incident, life treated them pretty well. The other children grew up, got married and had kids of their own. Ted eventually retired with a nice pension and he and Shirley led a quiet, peaceful life." Matt leaned forward and put his arms on the table, his voice deepening. "They were happily married for fifty-one years and they had loved each other every single day of that entire time. Then Shirley had a stroke. Ted had known her and had been close to her for nearly seventy years and suddenly she was gone from his life."

"Dude," Chris whispered.

"Yeah," Matt said and leaned back from the table. "Her loss nearly destroyed him. I never knew anyone could love another person so completely. I mean, I really felt his pain, Chris, just like he must have felt it. It was like my heart had been ripped right out of my chest and someone had just... *squeezed* it." He clenched his fist and held it out until it began to tremble with the intense emotion he was feeling.

"Yo, dude," Chris said, taking hold of his friend's hand and gently pressing it down onto the table. "Take it easy, now. These are someone else's memories, don't

135

forget."

Matt took a deep breath and slowly relaxed his hand. He looked down at the ring he wore and nodded. "Yeah, someone else. But, it felt so *real*. Like I was really living every minute of it—like I had some kind of connection to everything that happened back then."

"So, what else happened?" Chris asked, interested in spite of his earlier feelings.

"Well, Ted pretty much fell apart with Shirley gone. He had loved her for such a long time, he never recovered, really; it was like a huge part of his soul had been cut out and destroyed. The poor dude sank deeper and deeper into a depression and just gave up, I guess. Couldn't see going on without her by his side, so… well, he didn't."

"What do you mean?"

"He gave up on life," Matt said. "Just quit wanting to live and decided to join his wife."

"What, he died, too?"

"Lived less than a year after Shirley passed away."

"Jeez."

"And this is where the story gets weird," Matt told him.

"You mean it gets weird, *now?*" Chris asked, not trying to hide the sarcasm.

"Yeah," Matt said, with a crooked smile. "You know how much he loved her, right? I've mentioned that, haven't I?"

Chris just gave him a look, so he continued.

"So, Ted is lying on his deathbed, waiting to join his

beloved wife of more than fifty years and his oldest son
is there in the room with him. Ted is turning his
wedding ring around and around his finger—it's the
last physical contact he has with Shirley, you know?"
Chris nodded his head. "So, he tells his son that he
wants to be buried wearing his wedding ring, just like
she gave him, just like he buried Shirley with the one
she had. It was his dying wish." He paused for a
moment. "I guess some people think burying the dead
with jewelry is kind of a waste, you know—like
throwing money down the toilet or something."

Chris shrugged. "I never thought much about it."

"Guess you wouldn't think about it until someone
you cared about died."

"Yeah, I guess. Go on, dude."

"So, the son says, 'Sure, sure, whatever you want',
to appease the old man, but after Ted finally dies, he
slips the wedding ring off his finger, puts it in his
pocket and doesn't even tell anyone else about it."

"Shit."

"Right. So, Ted is buried next to Shirley, but without
his wedding ring. The son takes the ring home and
drops it in a box with his cuff links and clasps—crap
that he never wears any more and then just forgets
about it."

"You're kidding."

"No, dude. It sits there, completely ignored, for like
three years and all the while, Ted's spirit or whatever,
is wanting this ring back," Matt says, holding the ring
up for examination once again.

"So, how did you end up with it?"

"It gets even better. About a year ago, one of Ted's grandsons—the son of the guy who took the ring in the first place—is visiting his father's house. He finds Ted's wedding ring and doesn't even know what it actually is—he thinks it's just a plain old ring that belonged to his dad, but since he had never seen the old man wearing it, he figures his father would never miss it. And of course his father never did know it was gone, since he had forgotten about it almost as soon as he hid it away.

"So, the kid steals the ring and pawns all of Ted's memories for a lousy twenty bucks. It ends up in a display case for six months and then is sold in a lot with a bunch of gold rings and other crap to a wholesaler, who eventually sells it to the guy over at the Mine Shaft. And that's where I came into the story."

Chris whistled. "Incredible, dude. So, you got all of this drama from the ring, you think?"

Matt shrugged his shoulders and said, "I guess so."

Chris thought about everything he had heard for a minute, then asked, "Why do you think the ring picked you to unload all of these memories onto?"

"I'm not sure," Matt said, looking down at the thin band. "Maybe I was the first person to try the ring on after Ted died. Maybe I was just receptive enough to receive the memories." He shrugged, again. "I really have no idea."

"But… that's the end of the story, right?"

"Uh, no, not really," Matt said, quietly, looking up at Chris.

"What, you mean there's *more?*"

"Well, yeah. I mean, I'm pretty sure the ring showed me all of these very important, poignant memories for a reason, you know?"

"Like… for what reason?" Chris asked, warily.

"Well… I think Ted wants his ring back."

Chris shook his head and said, softly, "Dude, he's like dead and buried. How's he gonna get the ring back, now?"

Matt was quiet for a moment, then said, "Well, I was thinking we could give it to him."

Chris's eyes got very big. "We could take it out *where* to him?" he asked.

"To the cemetery, dude," Matt said and then grabbed at his friend's arm to keep him seated at the booth. "Wait, Chris, I'm serious about this."

Chris sat back down and Matt released his shirt sleeve. "Oh, no, no, no," Chris said and softly, "Dude, he's like dead and buried."

"I know he's dead, Chris," Matt said. "But I was shown all of his memories for a reason. Ted wanted me to know how much this ring meant to him and how important it was that he get it back. There's no other logical explanation."

"Logical?" Chris asked. "Now you want to suddenly be logical? It's a little bit late for that, don't you think?"

"What else can I do? If I don't get this ring back to him, it will drive me crazy, thinking about it every day."

Chris stared at his friend for some time, then finally shook his head, again. "Fine," he said, throwing his hands up in the air. Matt smiled and said, "No, dude, don't you smile at me like that. Even if we can find where they're buried—"

"Oh, I *know* where they're buried," Matt told him.

"Yeah, I forgot. Just how is it you know this, anyway?"

"I was at Shirley's funeral in the San Fernando Valley," he said, rather sadly. "With Ted, you know. I watched her being buried and I felt Ted's tears as he tried to say goodbye, but he just couldn't bring himself to really admit that she was gone."

"Okay, okay, I believe you. Sorry I brought it up. Again. So, once we get there, how do you propose to actually get the ring down to him?"

Matt stared at his hands and rubbed them together. "I… well… I'm not quite sure about that aspect of it."

"I'm not digging up any graves, dude, not even for you," Chris whispered, with rather intense feeling.

"No, no, I wasn't planning anything like that," Matt said, with that crooked smile of his. "I thought we could use some sort of a long, thin… something, to make a hole in the ground to drop the ring into. Maybe. That wouldn't get the ring all the way down to where he is, I know, but it might place it close enough to him to satisfy his spirit, or whatever it is that's sending me all of these memories."

Chris nodded, slowly. "That sounds sensible, I guess —as if any of this sounded sensible." He thought about it for a moment and said, "Hey, my dad went golfing a couple of weekends ago and you know what a lousy golfer he is." Matt smiled and nodded. "Anyway, he

140

came home with a few of his clubs, well, sort of damaged. I think a tree may have jumped out in front of him on the fairway or something. Strange shit like that happens to him when he goes golfing, you know?"

"Yeah."

"Anyway, one of the drivers was badly bent right where the head meets the shaft. We could take off the head and use the shaft to punch a hole in the ground like you wanted to do. The club is only about four feet long, but I don't know of anything else we might be able to use."

Matt nodded. "That sounds great. Do you think your dad would mind if we borrowed one of his clubs?"

"Naw. He tossed 'em in the corner of the garage when he got home from the links and they've been there ever since. I think he's given up the game. Again," he added with a grin.

"Great. Let's do it."

# # #

They stopped by Chris's house for the club—minus the head—and then took the freeway north. The ride took just over an hour and it was early evening by the time they turned into the cemetery gate.

"Okay," Chris said, as he drove slowly along the curving, narrow road, on either side of which timeworn headstones seemed to have sprouted at odd angles from the ground. This was an old cemetery, where large trees—oak, maple, pine and palm—

141

shaded the many paths and the varied, ornate headstones. "Where are they located, again?"

"Uh, somewhere near the back, I think."

"You think? I thought you knew where they were buried."

"Well, last time I was here, I was seeing this place through Ted's eyes, remember, and he was a little kid, at the time. It's near the back wall, somewhere. There were lots of old shade trees around."

"Oh, that's a big help," Chris muttered under his breath, as he steered the car toward the rear of the park.

"Look, Ted was an insurance broker. He knew the value of being prepared, so he bought these two plots right after they were married and got a really good deal on them, too, by the way."

"Great," Chris muttered.

"I mean, he picked out a really nice spot, at the back of the park on a low hill, so they would have a cool view of the entire cemetery."

Chris turned to stare at him. "Like, I'm sure the scenic view will be real important to the two of them, now."

"You know what I mean, dude," Matt said, surprised at his outburst.

"What's the matter with you, anyway?"

He turned his head back and said, "Sorry. I guess this whole thing is beginning to get to me. I'm not overly fond of cemeteries, okay?"

"Sure, no harm done. Just hang in there a few more minutes." Matt looked out the windshield and pointed.

"There, up there. See that little hill between the two big oak trees?" Chris nodded. "They're up there, between those trees. Stop over here."

Chris parked the car and they got out, Matt carrying the golf shaft close against his side, in case anyone noticed them. They moved up the low hill, to a ten-foot high fence of sun-baked stone and brick and there, nestled in the shade between the two towering oaks, a double headstone rested amidst thick grass several inches high. On a number of nearby graves, flowers — some still fresh, while some had seen better days — were lying on the grass or leaning against headstones. The two graves they approached, however, showed no sign of anyone having visited them in some time.

Chris stopped a few feet from the graves, but Matt moved forward to rest his hand on the chiseled marble of the headstone. He ran his fingers over the incised name in the stone. "Theodore 'Ted' Sterling," the inscription read. "Beloved husband and father." Shirley's name was carved into the stone next to Ted's.

"This is it," Matt said quietly. "Hey, Ted," he whispered to the stone, "I guess we've both been waiting for this meeting, eh?"

"C'mon, Matt," Chris said, anxiously. "Let's get this over with as quickly as possible, shall we?"

"All right," he agreed, turning from the headstone. "You keep an eye out and I'll get busy." Chris nodded and looked back to the road, watchful for anyone who might happen along and be curious as to why they were poking holes in someone's grave with a long stick.

Matt moved down a foot or so from Ted's headstone and placed the broken tip of the shaft against the dirt. The grounds here were well cared for and the earth was fairly soft beneath the grass. He leaned on the club and it sank slowly into the dirt. Pushing it down until just the handle was showing above the turf, Matt pulled the shaft out, then twisted it back and forth as it came up, to widen the hole just a bit.

"How we doing, Chris?" he asked, quietly, as he looked over his shoulder.

"So far, so good."

"Almost done," Matt told him. He removed the ring from his right hand and held it over the small hole. "Here you go, dude," he whispered. "I hope this will help you to find some peace, at last." Placing the ring just inside the opening, he used the remaining portion of the shaft to nudge it down as far as it would go into the ground. Removing the metal shaft, he filled in the barely noticeable hole with loose dirt and then stood, making sure the hole was completely covered by working grass and more dirt into it with his shoe.

Stepping back a few feet, Matt couldn't even see where the hole had been. "Okay, Chris. I'm finished."

"Great," he said, turning around. "Let's get the hell out of here."

Matt tossed him the shaft. "Go ahead. I'll be right along."

"Well, hurry up," Chris told him nervously, looking up at the sky. "It's like getting dark, dude." He turned and headed quickly toward the car.

Smiling, Matt went back and placed his right hand

on the headstone. The hand felt somewhat naked, now, without Ted's ring on his finger, but he was sure the band of gold was where it now belonged. It had been a difficult and bizarre week for him, but still, after everything he had been through, he thought that he might just miss having Ted's memories floating around in his head.

"Even though it was, well… really weird, thanks for letting me share a part of your life," he said, quietly, "for a little while, at least. Maybe I'll come by again and visit you and Shirley, when I have more time, if that's all right with you?"

A gentle breeze suddenly came out of nowhere to ruffle his hair and brush lightly against his cheek, then was gone as quickly as it appeared. Matt wasn't sure what had just happened, but wanted to think that gentle touch was somehow sent by the spirits of both Ted and Shirley, in way of thanks, so he whispered, "You're welcome."

He patted the cool, hard marble and turned away, but looked back after only a few steps. "You know, Ted," he added, "Shirley may have thought she loved you more than you loved her, but all things considered, I rather doubt it."

Matt gave a final nod toward the headstone and with a slightly crooked smile on his face, moved down the hill, to where Chris already had the car's engine running.

All That We See or Seem

...for Edgar Allan Poe

While this was the final story completed for this book, it was started some four years ago and sat dormant in my computer until just a few days before the manuscript was finished. The basis for the story is a recurring dream I have had for many, many years, but in my dream, I have never entered the house in question. What happens to the dreamer in this story is based on yet another episode in my life and although I survived my encounter with the creature mentioned herein, I was nevertheless emotionally damaged and this story thus serves as a warning to others.

I borrowed the title and a few lines of poetry for this story from the great master of the macabre, Edgar Allan Poe and so this story is dedicated to him, for "All that we see or seem is but a dream within a dream."

All That We See or Seem

THE HOUSE, AS always, beckoned to him.

For years he had been drawn to this house—in his dreams, in his nightmares. Although the all too familiar dream might start out with him in different, unknown locations, he always knew that he would be helplessly drawn in a certain direction, to eventually find himself standing on the cracked sidewalk before the old, abandoned house, wanting to enter, yet terrified to do so.

In the perpetual gloom of his mind, the house appeared gray, dormant and totally lifeless. Even so, the darkened windows, while unevenly boarded over, still seemed somehow silently watchful. This ancient, malevolent domicile gave the impression of being some aged, hulking beast, waiting patiently through the years for unsuspecting prey and he feared that if he

149

entered the house it would somehow devour him, completely.

§ § §

He had experienced this frightful, recurring dream dozens of times in his life, but this time it was different. Now, instead of being out on the sidewalk looking up in fear at the old house, he found himself actually standing on the sagging, wooden porch, just inches from the front door. Even as he willed himself not to, he reached for the knob, knowing the door would be unlocked. The house, as always, was waiting for him to enter.

Turning the knob, he pushed the door open, but let go of the tarnished brass handle as it swung slowly inward, for he could not yet bring himself to cross the threshold. The door opened slowly, with a high-pitched squeal of rusty, disused hinges and as light from the outside world spilled into the foyer, small patches of darkness seemed to scurry for the shadows. Sunlight, somehow faded by entering the surrounding gloom of the house, now littered the dust-covered floor. A gentle breeze stirred by the opening of the door enticed a frenzied dance of dust motes that suddenly spiraled up and then began to spin slowly through the stale air.

Hesitating as long as possible, he knew he must eventually enter, because something was waiting for him here—something that he both feared and longed for. Taking a deep breath, he stepped inside and as he did so, felt just the hint of a tainted breeze brush quickly past his face, almost as if the house had sighed.

The atmosphere within the house was dry and heavy with a mustiness that tasted of extreme age, as if the structure had stood empty and been undisturbed for many years. He smelled a distinct odor of decay and neglect that stung his nostrils and seemed to cake his throat with a dusty grit. He stood for a moment, allowing his eyes to adjust to the dimness, tasting the age of his surroundings.

The light from the open doorway did little to dispel the darkness toward the back of the hall, but as his eyes grew accustomed to the gloom, he could make out a narrow stairway about halfway down the right side, leading up into the darkness above. Dust shrouded cobwebs draped the banister and covered the darkly carpeted stairs, while portraits in faded frames of people long dead marched up the paneled wall next to the staircase. The oils of the paintings were cracked and dimmed with age, leaving the features indistinct. Only the eyes still seemed clear and defined and they appeared to glow balefully in the feeble light. Cobwebs sagging under the weight of age dripped from the frames to the stairs and carpet below.

Tearing his sight away from those eyes staring at him from the paintings, he saw to his right a pair of closed, sliding doors. On the other side of the hall was another pair of sliding doors, which stood part way open. The narrow opening between these doors was blocked by a thick curtain of aged, dusty cobwebs. Moving to the doorway, he brushed away the still sticky strands and turned sideways to enter the room, so he would not have to touch the doors themselves. Through two partially boarded windows, weak sunlight managed to poorly illuminate the room where he now stood. This must have been a parlor, he decided; an overstuffed couch and a pair of matching chairs crouched within the small, crowded room, in front of a cold, dark, fireplace. In one corner, a thin ray of sunlight fell upon a small table, next to a wing-back chair. On the table lay an open book, light from the nearby window spilling over its pages. Curious, he moved to the table and looked down at the book. Years of dust had coated the age-yellowed pages and he wiped a section of one page clean with his thumb, reading the faded words that he exposed.

"I stand amid the roar
Of a surf-tormented shore,
And I hold within my hand
Grains of golden sand—
How few! Yet how they creep
Through my fingers to the deep,
While I weep—while I weep!"

He shuddered, involuntarily, even as he recognized the work as part of a poem by Edgar Allan Poe. Something about a dream within a dream—he couldn't quite remember. It was then that he heard a creak of wood from somewhere out in the hallway. He moved quickly back to the parlor entrance, sidled between the doors and stood in the middle of the hall, ready to bolt out the front door, if need be. Looking carefully around the entry hall, he saw nothing amiss, but even as his heart slowed its panicked thumping, he felt as if he were being watched. Raising his eyes to the stairway, he looked slowly up to the narrow balcony at the top of the stairs and his breath caught in his throat.

A dim figure stood there in the near darkness of the upper hall, staring down at him. This was the girl he had seen so many times in his dreams—she whom he had seen after so many nights, through so many nightmares, but had never quite been able to reach. She was dressed in a floor-length, strapless, red satin gown, her bare arms and shoulders pale white against the darkness. The long, heavy black ringlets of her hair were almost invisible against the darkened background, except where they touched her face and brow. Her face too was pale; so very pale it carried the ghostly pallor of death about it. Only the deep, bloody crimson of her slightly parted lips and the ice-cold blue of her eyes added a hint of stark color to the skin.

She stared down at him for a few seconds, her intense gaze freezing his soul. Those eyes—they bespoke of such wondrous pleasure, and such unthinkable pain. The very sight of her triggered in his mind myriad thoughts of carnal lust and he began to tremble in both anticipation—and in fear. Holding him thus enthralled for another few heartbeats, she suddenly looked away and he nearly collapsed as she released her magnetic grasp on him. Then she slowly turned and trailing a red, satin-gloved hand along the banister, seemed to float gracefully down the hall, out of his sight.

The spell of her presence now broken, he raised a

hand and almost called out to her, but then realized that would avail him nothing. If he wanted her, he would have to follow her. That was what she wanted him to do, after all; he must follow her more deeply into the house. That was what the house wanted. That was why he was here. She was the bait in this trap and he knew that he was helplessly hooked.

He recognized her now, knew her for what she truly was—a Succubus: that breed of vile demon which sought out men while they slept and savagely ravished them, seeking to drain their very life force, often to death. But, curiously, that knowledge still did not keep him from painfully wanting her. Yet he hesitated, knowing full well that if he gave in to the cravings that goaded him on, it might well mean his ultimate doom. Slowly, with a mighty force of will, he took a step backwards, toward the still open front door, not daring to take his eyes off the indistinct shadows of the balcony. A part of him feared that she might reappear and knew that if she did, he would have to follow her, and yet, still another part of him *wanted* to see her again—*needed* to see her again. His very soul ached for just one more, single, brief glimpse of her, even as he took another step slowly backwards, away from her and toward freedom.

Feeling sunlight caressing the backs of his legs as he moved into the welcome warmth near the door, he froze again, hearing his name—*so close!* But, now he listened intently for another sound from the balcony. He took a halting step forward, his movements no longer under his control and heard the light sound of laughter from above.

"Come to me, my darling," her voice whispered beneath the soft laughter and he was helpless to defy that command.

He shuffled, stiff legged, slowly toward the stairs and moaned, softly, as her mirthless laughter drifted down to him. The thick barrier of cobwebs draped across the stairs attempted to impede his progress, but he pushed stiffly through them, his gaze locked on the balcony above. His legs trembling from the exertion, he continued to climb the steep stairway, feeling the watchful eyes of the nearby portraits boring into his soul as he slinked past them.

Panting, he at last reached the balcony and clutching the banister, turned to look down the hallway. At the far end, a partly opened door allowed faint light to enter the passage, showing a deep pall of dust covering the floor. No footprints appeared in that deep coating and a veil of gently swaying, unbroken cobwebs crisscrossed the hall, but *she* had just passed this way, yet left no indication that anything had recently moved by. Still, he *felt* her waiting for him, just beyond that open door.

On legs grown suddenly numb, he stumbled down the hall, brushing the suffocating cobwebs from his face as he pushed through them, puffs of stagnant, ageless dust ballooning up around his feet as he moved toward… what? He did not know why he moved forward, only that he was compelled to do so. Knowing vaguely that his doom awaited him, he also knew that the pleasure which would precede his demise would be well worth any pain he might suffer —or so he thought.

He stopped before the door, breathing heavily, filled with apprehension and longing. He knew he could actually *smell* her presence—a thick, cloying stink of putrescent decay, but mixed, somehow, with the compelling, lustful scent of sex. Unable to stop himself, he pushed open the door and looked upon her lair. Discovering the room to be empty, he found himself close to tears, whether due to relief or disappointment, he could not tell.

With a deep sigh, he entered the dimly lit room and looked about himself. He stood in a large, obviously long-disused bedroom. As with all else in this house, dust and aged cobwebs covered everything, though there was a single candle flickering on a low table next to an oversized bed that occupied most of the room. The bedcover had rotted down to bare wood and yellowed sheets with curious, crusted dark stains upon them were exposed, a thin layer of dust covering the lot. Near the door, a chest of drawers stood against one wall and he moved over to it, cautiously opening the narrow, top drawer.

Inside was a layer of sleek, colorful undergarments, surprisingly devoid of dust and appearing to be fresh and pristine. Curious, he slipped his hands into the slinky pile of satin panties and lace-edged slips and lifted them to his face, rubbing the cool, smooth, slick fabric against his tortured, fevered skin. He buried his face within the soft material which was filled with her fragrant essence, and drank deeply the secret scents of sex and lust hidden therein. As he hungrily inhaled her dusky aroma, a strong, unexpected stirring erupted within his loins and he moaned in anguish, the weak sound muffled by the silken mound of cloth against his mouth.

Tinkling, liquid laughter from behind him froze his thoughts and he slowly turned. She was sprawled lazily back on the bed, one knee lifted so the hem of her dress had fallen back revealing an expanse of pale thigh and a triangle of dark promise between her legs. Her black hair fanned out across the pillow, one arm behind her head, those ice cold eyes glinting in the candle light. A dark tongue slid out and moistened thick, blood red lips which curved up into a sinister smile. Her ample, swelling breasts heaved beneath the tight, satin covering of the dress; small, hard points which were her nipples strained against the material and quivered with her rapid breathing.

His attention riveted on her unhealthy presence, he dropped the handful of undergarments he held, not noticing that they crumbled into stained bits of moldy, dusty material as they fell from his grasp. Whimpering in agony and burning with a fever only her diseased contact could quench, he staggered over to the bed, his uncontrollable, painful desire now swelling the contour of his pants.

Eyeing his obvious need, the cracked lips of her smile broadened, revealing sharpened, yellow teeth. She held out pale, thin arms to him, as cracked and broken talons erupted from the tips of her fingers. Helplessly drawn to her, even though knowing his end was near, he knelt on the bed and allowed her to pull him down, to press his heated, trembling body against her own, frigid corpse. As her sharpened claws raked the flesh of his naked back, he cried out and thrust forcefully into her, the searing pain of his body being ripped asunder mingled with an exquisite and unimaginable pleasure as she sank her pointed, decaying teeth deeply into his neck.

He felt a flush of hot blood disgorge from his groin, as well as from his neck, and even as his seed exploded for one final time, he knew she had won. His climax rocked them both and the ancient bedsprings creaked and sang in protest as his body fought the violence of her embrace. He howled in fatal, defeated anguish, even as the creature beneath him cackled in undisguised triumph, drinking in the last of his spent life force, hungrily slurping up each and every drop that poured forth.

The unbearable pain, he realized too late, had not, after all, been worth the transient pleasure, but it was far too late to alter his decision. His brain burned with flame, the very cells of his body cried out in torment and, as his soul was engulfed in utter darkness and pain, he heard her faint laughter, one final time to underscore his ultimate loss. Tears welled up in his eyes, but they evaporated quickly in the unrelenting heat and he felt himself falling away from her fatal grasp, falling forever into the burning darkness...

§ § §

They found him several days later, lying in his bed, long dead, with his face in a frozen rictus of unimaginable pain and terror. It was obvious to the investigating detectives that he had died in his bed, but they could not explain, in an otherwise clean and well appointed room, the thick layer of aged dust that coated his feet and legs, nor how or why his naked body and tormented face were covered with dried and dusty cobwebs.

The End

About the Author

Terry D. Scheerer
(September 26, 1949 – February 2, 2016)
Also known as: L. Craig Woods, Zed Holt, MOK, Reaper Rick

Terrence Dean Wall, best known by his pen name *Terry D. Scheerer*, was a prolific American writer, editor, poet, film producer, podcaster, and executive, whose creative work spanned across dark fantasy, horror, science fiction, and gothic fiction. He left behind a legacy of deeply personal storytelling, powerful editorial vision, and tireless support for the independent creative community.

Early Life and Personal Struggles

Born in Carthage, Missouri, on a dark and stormy night in 1949, Terry would often reflect on the stormy conditions of his birth as symbolic of the tone his life would take. He was moved to Southern California at age two by his mother and grandmother, he was raised in Long Beach under the shadow of a dysfunctional family. A solitary and introverted child, Terry found solace in literature, music, and the vivid world of his imagination. By age eleven, he was writing stories, which became a lifelong outlet for his internal struggles.

Terry faced mental health battles early on, experiencing depression and suicidal ideation as a teenager. Despite finding momentary stability through therapy and medication, his struggle with chronic depression remained a lifelong companion. He drifted through college in the late 1960s—initially majoring in art before switching to biological sciences—and earned good grades in subjects he loved but struggled in others.

Drafted during the Vietnam War in 1971, he was deemed unfit for overseas service due to high blood pressure. With a young family to support, he left college just shy of a degree following the death of his grandmother and turned to the medical field, earning a degree in respiratory therapy, he worked in hospitals for over a decade, constantly exposed to terminal illness, which which deepened his emotional strain.

Writing Career and Rise to Prominence

Though he wrote intermittently for years, Terry's professional writing career didn't blossom until the late 1990s. He submitted stories to online magazines such as *Dragon's Laugh* and *SwordsEdge*, and by the early 2000s had gained traction as a dark fantasy author. In 2003, his short story "The Dragon Hunters" was published in *Sword's Edge*, beginning a prolific stretch of published work. He was inspired by writers such as H.P. Lovecraft, Robert E. Howard, and Vaughn Bodē.

In 2005, Terry self-published his breakout collection *Dreams of Darkness, Dreams of Night* through his own company, **Gateway Press**, combining poetry and short stories that reflected his battles with depression, grief, and existential dread. The book was followed by *The Dragon Hunters and Other Fantasy Tails* in 2011, and dozens of published works in magazines such as *The World of Myth, GlassFire*, and *Horrotica*.

His widely praised story "Between the Moon and Mars" won a short story award in 2004, cementing his place in the indie literary world.

Editorial Influence and Executive Leadership

In 2004, Terry joined **Dark Myth Production Studios**, where he became Editor-in-Chief of *The World of Myth Magazine*. Known for his eye for raw talent and his supportive approach, he gave new voices a platform and guided them with care. In 2007, he also became Editor-in-Chief of *Horrotica Magazine*.

Terry's leadership extended beyond editing. By

2011, he was promoted to *Chief Operating Officer* of Dark Myth, overseeing operational strategy, publication planning, and editorial alignment across multiple divisions. He was a driving force behind *The Horrotica Magazine Anthology*, which he considered his swan song, and it marked his retirement from publishing in 2012.

Filmmaking and Podcasting

Never content to stay in one medium, Terry ventured into film production in 2012. He worked with **Creep Creepersin** to produce several indie films, including *Paranormal Ghost Hunters Case Files, Awesome Girl Gang Street Fighter, Dracula*, and *Gritty*.

In 2013, Terry transitioned into podcasting under the name **Reaper Rick**. His shows *Scheerer Darkness, News, Views and Reviews*, and *Reaper Rick's Tree Frog Exposé Café* combined dark humor, cultural commentary and film reviews. Despite health issues that led to inconsistent appearances, he remained a fan-favorite voice on iTunes, where his shows briefly cracked the Top 100.

Final Years and Legacy

Terry's final years were marked by continued health battles. Diagnosed with prostate cancer in 2005, he underwent multiple treatments over a decade. In 2010, he suffered a severe car accident that left him hospitalized and learning to walk again. In 2014, complications from diabetes and high blood pressure led to renal failure. A year later, he suffered a stroke that permanently took his voice, officially ending his creative career.

TERRY D. SCHEERER

On February 2, 2016, Terry D. Scheerer passed away peacefully in his sleep in Apple Valley, California, at the age of 66.

Legacy and Bibliography

Terry D. Scheerer left behind a staggering body of work, including over 75 published stories, multiple anthologies, and several editorial milestones. His most notable works include:

- *Dreams of Darkness, Dreams of Night (2005)*
- *The Dragon Hunters and Other Fantasy Tails* (2011)
- *Queen of the Westerlands* (2005–2010, serialized in The World of Myth)
- *Between the Moon and Mars* (2004)

He was not just a writer but a mentor, a builder of creative communities, and an advocate for indie voices. His legacy lives on through the stories he told and the people he inspired.